IN LOVE WITH A SHE-WOLF

A Lesbian Erotica Retelling of Beauty and the Beast

Mickey Gatz

CONTENTS

In Love
With
A
She-Wolf

PROLOGUE

Years Ago.

Every night she prowled a graceful beast, slashing the night air with her long bushy tail like a gifted swordsman slicing through the invisible air with his sword. The girl could see the beast's lean hairy but oddly seductive flanks as she growled, her paws taping the royal castle grounds in an even pattern, when the beast flashed her coal red eyes at the girl and let out a howl, the whole castle cowered with fear but sitting in the castle garden the girl stretched out her hands to the beast without fear for they were lovers, woman, and beast, an unprecedented love soiree, can you beat that?? But that's the love they found, you shall soon understand when you hear my story. Meanwhile, the wolf howled her way towards the girl, stepped daintily over the garden flowers, and stood firmly before the girl stopped her blood-curdling howl. For several seconds the beast considered the girl's outstretched hands, the girl watched the wolf's face relax into a beastly smile, without much ado the beast stepped into the girl's arms and started to whimper in the enjoyment of the moment and because of the gruesome pain she daily had to suffer, the girl gently fingered the soft furs of the beast and closed her eyes with a mixture of mild fear and anticipated Sweetness as the beast opened her Jaws, revealed her gleaming teeth and took the girl's white tender breast into her great Jaws, the girl collapsed into the roses, enjoying the moment.

BOOK ONE

CHAPTER ONE

THE FEAST ON VIRGINS

5. Stroking the tender nipples

Creating a delicious ripple

between her legs and making her cackle

The mad lover put his erect spindle

into the moist quivering temple

10. A feast on virgins

Carnal exploits intoxicating as gin.

He stroked the firm thighs of the naive young beauty, traced a wet kiss from the hollow in between her breasts down to her navel, the young beauty quivered with excitement and asked for more, the man slid his long fingers into her and found her tight, he grinned with excitement and absolute enjoyment at the discovery, she was indeed a virgin. That made him go crazy, he removed his royal robe hurriedly, kicked off his pants quickly like the demons of hell were after him, the young beauty wished he would hurry up and continue with the delicious sensation he was cooking on her body, he finally kicked off the troublesome pants and pounced on the young beauty who was already licking her lips in anticipation. She closed her eyes as he covered her pretty face with kisses, her skin was as perfect as coral, as white as though she washed with milk so he took his time kissing every inch of her, from her forehead to her eyes, and hurried back to her ears, the sensation he created in her ears made her mew like a cat, she clung her naked body to his naked body creating a natural electrical spark, very quickly he took his kisses down to her throat then back to her chubby baby-like rosy cheeks, she gasped when he covered her small young breast with his mouth, sucking mercilessly on her pink nipples, that was too much for her so she screamed. Her moans were like pouring fuel on a raging fire, he was mad with passion and she was reckless with desire. Taking his time, he sucked her breasts like a hungry baby, the Sweetness was more than she could bear so though it was her first time in bed with a man she boldly reached down and grabbed him, he was hard, big, and very warm, she involuntarily gasped, wondering if she could contain the whole length of him, while she thought of the sweet-pain ahead of her, he took his length from her palms and stroked it, smiling wickedly down at the girl and without warning her plunged in. She was so tight so he took his time stretching her, the girl screamed and her voice was heard in the whole royal castle but no one dared intervene for her merciless lover was no other person than the duke of Zazu, the imperial monarch of one the greatest empires on earth, he was ruthless in his reign and his subjects feared him, he was rumored to be very gentle only when in bed with pretty women. His name is Gastard, the Duke of Zazu kingdom, he sat on the throne of his father after the death of his parents the late Gastard Snr and his queen Annabella, they both died of the terrible flu and according to the sacred custom of the Zazu empire, Gastard Jnr took over the royal ancestral stool of the Gastard dynasty. He had only one sister, an astonishingly pretty princess called Nirvana. Not only was Gastard an imperial Duke, but he was also the wealthiest in his time, in those days when the earth was divided into kingdoms and Dukedoms, those days when magic roamed free, Zazu empire was the greatest of them all, an empire blessed with inexhaustible gold, a prosperous city flowing with milk and honey. Hence, though Gastard was a ruthless king, the people had enough riches as consolation. So while he ruled with an iron fist and feasted on virgins of the empire like a dog, the people of Zazu looked at the sumptuous riches around them and were consoled. Therefore while the young beauty screamed under the merciless lovemaking of Gastard, no man born of a woman could intervene, the whole royal castle shook with the pleasure they shared in the king's private chambers yet no man dared run to her rescue, not even Winthrop, who stood outside the golden door of the king's chamber could intervene, he was one of the king's guards and daily suffered the torture of hearing the king having his pleasure with the prettiest damsels of the land while the poor Winthrop had the unfortunate task of listening to the loud moans of the women as Gastard stroked them to paradise. To make matters worse, those women were all screamers so Winthrop suffered countless erections without release, he would painfully listen to the king's enjoyment, hide his erections under his flowing robe and run to the servants quarters after the king dismissed him to find Annie, the palace kitchen maid who was always eager to spread her legs. Annie was kind, willing, and sweet in the right places. For over an hour the king had his pleasure and at the snap of his fingers, Winthrop knew it was over so he gathered the numerous bars of gold that would be used to compensate the young beauty. Winthrop entered Gastard's chambers just as Gastard was ordering the young beauty out of his bed. Yea, that was classic Gastard at his best, he would have his pleasures with his ladies, after satisfying himself he would order them out of his bed, the ladies were always shocked at the dramatic change in his mood for he was always kind and loving before he had his way but then despite their shock these ladies always ran off his bed fearing his rage for Gastard was tall, lean as a rake, with large eyes that always sparkled with rage, his nose was almost as long as Pinocchio's yet he managed to be handsome a handsome royal jerk. The young beauty scampered off his large bed decorated with royal carvings from India, the bedspread was the soft expensive Egyptian bed sheets but the red hot rage in Gastard's eyes didn't let the young beauty admire any of these, she grabbed the gold from Winthrop and ran off forgetting her bonnet, she ran to her father's house not looking back even once. At her departure Gastard smiled wickedly enjoying himself immensely, that was over and done with so he licked his lips and waited for the next woman while Winthrop poured his favorite wine. A mild commotion was heard at the gates of the castle but Gastard wasn't worried because he was expecting it. The Lords of the empire had already written him a note that they wanted his audience, even before their arrival Gastard knew what they were going to say, they had said the same thing over the years repeatedly so why don't they just give up Gastard asked himself. He was sure that once again they were going to ask him when he was going to marry, it was generally believed that when he found a queen he would leave the virgins of the empire alone, the virgins of Zazu were fast running out, a thing unheard of in other kingdoms. Gastard just had to marry the Lord's chosen. Secondly, they were going to ask about the whereabouts of princess Nirvena who since last winter was missing and was not seen again, the whole empire was worried about her strange disappearance. The knights of Zazu, those gallant soldiers of the Zazu empire searched for the princess under the falling snow all through last winter yet nothing was seen of her. Thirdly the Lords were going to plead with the Duke to kindly stop creating trouble with other kingdoms, before the disappearance of princess Nirvena, Zazu was thrown into dire peril when king Arthur, the grand king of a neighboring kingdom threatened to declare war on Zazu, king Arthur's rage was such that he threatened to turn his dreaded sorcerer Merlin loose on Zazu, to make matters worse, king Arthur's rage was justified for he threatened war because Gastard deflowered his sister Morgana, no one could explain how the Duke of Zazu found his way into princess Morgana's bed right under the nose of King Arthur but that was the kind of sexual miracles Gastard performed at the expense of his kingdom. Princess Nirvena saved the day when she, escorted by the finest knights of Zazu, rode under the cover of darkness amid the thick snow to the castle of King Arthur, of course, they were immediately seized until Princess Nirvena started her mission. She was offering herself to king Arthur in exchange for the life of her people. King Arthur was speechless with shock, he never thought the cheeriest apple of Zazu would one day grace his bed. He had dreamt of dancing in between her legs and suddenly she was at his mercy and asking him to make his dreams come true. King Arthur roamed his eyes from the full succulent breast of princess Nirvena down to her trim waist, the falling snow had drenched her so her robe clung to her body seductively, king Arthur could see the triangle in between her legs, he swallowed hungrily and shook his head like the agama lizard, the war he intended to wage was forgotten, he took princess Nirvena to his private chambers and explored the paradise she had to offer. King Arthur danced in between her legs like he had imagined in his head, he thrust into her with enjoyment like a child set loose in a candy store. Princess Nirvena's hips danced involuntarily to the music king Authur played, her breasts were on fire for he ate them like ripe apples. All of these princess Nirvena bore for the sake of her people, she was irritated at king Arthur's touch for he wasn't the lover she wanted though he was very good looking. That she had given her virginity to save her people from the magic portions of Merlin made her shed silent tears as king Arthur ate the sugar in between her legs. The kings were even and the war was completely forgotten, Zazu finally had peace. Oh!!! The Lords had a lot to say to Gastard, they were going to ask him what he planned to do about the she-wolf that recently started prowling the empire, a strange beast that prowled when the clock struck the midnight hour, it maimed any man confronting her sparing only the women. Gastard knew the Lords of Zazu were going to drill him with questions and wished he could avoid the meeting especially as he was seriously contemplating on how to bring to his bed the prettiest Zazu maiden he ever saw, a maiden he saw some days ago, she was like the Greek goddess of beauty Aphrodite. His inquiries revealed that the maiden is the fairest of all ladies in Zazu, in all the kingdoms and across the vast seas. She was called Claire.

CHAPTER TWO

5. She spread her legs

exposing the shiny triangle shiny as keg

He fingered the temple till it was red

begging her for a wider spread

10. Together they built ecstasy

Indulging their bedroom fantasies

The meeting of the Zazu Lords with Gastard was frustrating because while Lord Henry listed out the problems of the empire, it was obvious to the Lords that the Duke wasn't even listening and truly he wasn't. Gastard kept staring into space, lost in his inglorious thoughts. While Lord Henry explained the empire's problems, Gastard was busy mentally creating pictures of what he was going to do with Claire when his guards finally traced her. He thought of how he was going to gently tap her bouncy arse and bite her full breasts until her nipples turned red. As he was thinking it, he developed a big erection, so big that Lord Henry who was standing before his throne noticed it and turned red with embarrassment. Gastard did his best to cover his embarrassment with his voluminous robe but the erotic scenes in his head were so vivid that his erection stayed strong. His Lords were within seconds pointing at it, Lord Henry hurriedly took his seat for he was unspeakably embarrassed. The Lords were torn between laughter and annoyance so while some of them laughed in absolute enjoyment of the situation, the others were too angry to laugh. One of the lords, a fearless man called William respectfully bowed before the Duke and told him to his face that he the Duke was a disappointment to the empire, Zazu was in dire danger and he the Duke of the empire was busy entertaining an erection in full view of the Royal Court. The other Lords feared for the safety of Lord William, they knew Gastard wasn't a Duke to tolerate corrections from anyone irrespective of who was giving it and the validity of the correction being given. Before Gastard said a word, it was obvious to all the Lords in court that Lord William had dug his grave. Just as expected, Gastard snapped his fingers and at the same instant, Winthrop and two other guards came in, Gastard ordered them to take Lord William away. The courageous Lord was rudely dragged out of the royal court like a common criminal but that wasn't enough for classic Gastard, he whispered to Winthrop that he wanted the busty wife of Lord William on his bed that evening, she was to be carried to the castle if she refused to come obediently. The Lords saw the Duke whispering something to the guard but were unable to decode the content of the conversation. Perhaps if they had known, they would have pleaded on behalf of William. It was bad enough to humiliate a man for speaking the truth, abducting his wife, and forcefully licking the orange in between her legs is just unacceptable, frankly abominable but the Duke was past caring. At the exit of the guards, the meeting continued but on a sober note, the Lords were sorely discouraged and wished the devil would just take the dreadful Duke to hell but wishes are not horses and beggars can't ride. The drama of the moment managed to demolish the erection that started the whole hullabaloo and the meeting progressed. Gastard stood to his full six- feet - plus height and assured the Lords that he had heard their complaints and was going to do his best to return the empire to normalcy. The Lords were unimpressed, even a baby could tell that the words of the Duke were empty promises. Dukes in those days were untouchable, they were seen as demi-gods to whom the people must give maximum respect and allegiance. Therefore, though Gastard promises were as good as nothing, the Lords respectfully bowed and retired to the royal banquet hall to be entertained.

The news of Lord William's arrest was spread throughout the whole empire, his wife wept uncontrollably, perhaps if she knew what was coming she would have fled that instant. Her two little daughters did not understand the happenings in the family, they simply saw their mother crying and cried with her. Lady William put her two little daughters to bed as the day grew darker, the little girls had just had dinner, as lady William tucked them into bed, they kept asking about daddy, their mother had no ready answer so she merely smiled while trying hard to control her tears. Then the knock came, a heavy rude knock that brought lady William out of bed, when the maid of the Williams opened the door, she screamed in fright. Standing at the door were two fierce-looking royal guards, she had never seen them at close range before so she was immensely frightened. The maid was pushed out of the way, but one of the guards named Gerrard looked at the maid's behind and discovered she had a bouncy arse, he was pleasantly surprised and took the opportunity to squeeze the arse of the girl. The maid was too scared to complain but gave him a scornful look which turned out to be a mistake because Gerrard drew her closer and squeezed her young breast while the girl screamed. Lady William took the stairs two at a time, she entered her opulent sitting room and saw the two royal guards, one was sitting arrogantly on her chair, while the other, a tall, fierce-looking man with the muscles of a wrestler was naughty liberties with her maid. Lady William's heart sank with fear into her stomach, before she could say a word, her maid ran behind her for protection while the guards told her that her presence was needed at the royal castle. She had heard stories of Gastard and she knew what he did to women. Without thinking, she turned and started running back upstairs, the guards were amused by her performance, her maid taking a cue from her run from the sitting room like a pursued rodent. Gerrard took two long strides and captured Lady William, her struggles amused the guards, even more, they hauled her into the royal carriage and rode off. Lady William's children drawn by the noise downstairs came down, their mother was nowhere to be seen, the door leading outside was wide open, the little girls were bewildered and in unison started wailing, meanwhile at the castle, Gastard waited impatiently for his prey. Within minutes, the guards and their prey arrived at the castle. Gerrard bundled lady William to the Duke's private chamber while the other guard took the carriage horses to their stable. Gastard in seeing lady William smiled wickedly while lady William glared at him with hatred. Gastard dismissed the guard with a wave of his hand, he told lady William that it was her husband's smart mouth that landed her in his private chamber, when lady William said nothing, Gastard was enraged. With one swift movement, he tore lady William's night cloth off her body. Though a mother of two, she still wore seductive undies and Gastard was impressed. He slowly circled the woman, wordlessly admiring her, her hips were perfectly rounded and her breasts were as big as coconuts, Gastard licked his lips repeatedly, he didn't see why he shouldn't enjoy himself meanwhile lady William shed silent tears. The terrible Duke was inspecting her glory and enjoying himself, she wished she could just kill him. Within minutes Gastard wrestled his prey into his majestic bed, at first she struggled wildly but Gastard's fingers were firmly inside her honey pot, the more she fought the harder he stroked, against her will she heard herself moaning, Gastard smiled, he had her just where he wanted her. He pulled her against his erection and sucked her large rounded breasts, Lady William's eyes were closed in ecstasy, she couldn't believe she was enjoying the moment. From one full breast, he moved to the other, sucking noisily like a naughty child while stroking her honey pot with all the tenderness he could afford. Lady William in a fit of passion bit his shoulder but that didn't stop Gastard, he saw that bite as a gift of love though his shoulder burned. He spread her legs widely, put a hand beneath her hip, and entered her fully and completely. For several seconds lady, William was stunned for he was so big, bigger than her husband, her honey pot hadn't been so filled before, she never even knew it was possible and so against her will she moved her hips hungrily, urging him to take her to the night cloud that moment, Gastard only obeyed the women in his bed so very obediently he started to do his magic, he took her like he was going to die that night, lady William forgot completely that her husband was Gastard's prisoner and matched his thrusts tirelessly. They sweated the night away, round after round. She was so sweet that Gastard kept her the whole night, he had intended to send her home later that night but decided against it. He wanted the full round breasts on his face all night and he liked the way lady William's hips rose to meet his thrusts, he liked women who could bounce on a man's erection and lady William was a good bouncer. When they were done, a fruit wine from Zazu's finest distillery and barbecue was brought by Winthrop, cuddled together they drank and toasted to an amazing night, completely forgetting that Lord William was in a cold cell in the castle prison. As the clock struck twelve, a faint noise was heard in the stillness of the night, Gastard and his lover knew that the beast was on the prowl again and was being attacked by the knights of Zazu on night patrol. They were perfectly safe in the vast chamber of the king, so they could afford to have another round of passion while some unfortunate knights fought the beast. The next morning, courtesy of the excellent performance of Lady William, Lord William was set free to the astonishment of the whole empire, they didn't expect him to get off so light, if only they knew the price Lady William paid. Just like her predecessors, Lady William was ordered out of bed the next morning to her astonishment, how could her passionate lover of yesternight turn so cold but like her predecessors she hurriedly wore her robe and ran as fast as her legs could carry her. Two days later, there were rumors that Lord William had divorced his wife, he was told by a palace maid that while he was in prison his wife was brought to the castle. When he questioned his wife, lady William made the mistake of smiling, that wasn't intentional, she just couldn't help it, the memory of that night's escapade with Gastard was so sweet that she smiled before she could stop herself. That was all the confirmation Lord William needed, he quickly sent her packing and the whole of Zazu was aflame with the news. That was the kind of drama Gastard created, he feasted on virgins and wrecked marriages without stopping to think twice.

CHAPTER THREE

5. She is sweeter than honey

For she offers pleasures pricier than money

In his arms soft and comely

She makes him hard and horny

10. A trip to cloud nine

I thrust hard and make her mine

One afternoon, barely one week after the drama of Lady William and the Duke, Claire the prettiest damsel across all kingdoms was at the great Zazu Market helping her mother in her store. Her mother produced perfumes at the Zazu market and was quite popular because of the quality of her perfumes. Claire was about to head home when some palace guards bounced into her mother's store, they took her mother aside and spoke for several minutes with her. The attention of everyone at the market was drawn to the exchange between Claire's mother and the guards, Gastard's reputation was such that whenever his guards approached any girl or any family that had a pretty damsel, the whole empire knew why. So when the guards were speaking to Claire's mother, a lot of people became very sorry for Claire, they knew without any doubt that the Duke was going to dance in between her legs, she was the fairest of all damsels, it was almost inevitable that Gastard would come for her. They only wished Claire found a better man, not the dog who called himself the Duke. Claire herself was already close to tears, she could see herself losing her virginity in no distant time, the worry and fear on her mother's face confirmed that all wasn't well at all. During the conversation, Claire attempted to escape but a keen-eyed guard glared at her wickedly and she stayed put. The second the conversation ended, Claire's mother ran to her daughter and pulled her into a tight hug, Claire felt some wetness on her shoulder and knew her mother was crying, that was all she needed to cry herself but the guards were impatient, they needed to report back to the Duke who was waiting impatiently for his Claire. When Claire's mother made move to release her, the guards gently pulled her away from her mother, a lot of people at the market had tears in their eyes though they tried hard to mind their business. The prettiest girl in the kingdom was going to dance on the Duke's ever-hard dick and they were naturally sorry for her. Claire with eyes filled with tears was put in a royal carriage and taken to the castle, she cried all the way, at a point the guards felt sorry for her but it wasn't in their power to set her free so onwards they moved. On getting to the palace, Winthrop informed the guards that Claire was to be taken to the private dining hall of the Duke, the guards were mildly surprised, they were used to sending every damsel they brought to the castle straight to the Duke's bed-chamber, that the Duke was going to entertain Claire was a deviation from his normal practice. Claire was taken to the private dining hall of the Duke and got the shock of her life. There she saw the finest and most sumptuous meals she had ever seen in her life, the floors of the hall were decorated with Persian rugs, the dining hall chairs were of gold with exquisite carvings on the chair, the most shocking thing was the Duke himself, for the first time Claire was seeing him without rage in his eyes, he even had a friendly seductive smile on his face. For several seconds the Duke was lost in admiration, from the first day he saw Claire he knew she was beautiful but on a closer look, she was breath-taking with blond hair that flowed in waves beyond her bouncy arse, her skin sparkled white as alabaster. Though her face was streaked with tears yet her massive beauty could not be hidden, her face was oval-shaped with beautiful eyes that were soft and dreamy, her lashes were thick and long shadowing her very blue eyes, blue as the sky. Looking at Claire's eyes, Gastard felt he was looking at the sky and loved it immensely, he started shifting excitedly on his seat like a child presented with a fabulous toy. Claire was frightened at the Duke's uncontrolled admiration but Gastard didn't let that discourage him, he took his time to study the sensual curve of her lips, the fullness and firmness of her breast and her very flat tummy, her hips were perfectly rounded, too perfectly rounded for such a slim girl and oh!! those breasts, Gastard assumed her breasts were pointing at him. So he decided he was going to take several minutes to suck on those breasts since according to him they pointed at him. Claire was petite and perfect, just the kind he loved, a petite astonishing beauty he could flip into different positions in bed. He licked his lips severally and invited Claire to the dining table. The royal chefs stood respectfully at the corners of the dining hall awaiting the Duke's orders. At a signal from Gastard, they approached the table and started serving the three-course buffet they prepared for the Duke's special guest, Claire's eyes roamed the table and saw all the delicacies she loved, most were so expensive that her father who was a gardener in the castle couldn't afford to buy them. There were perfectly barbecued salmons, barbecued turkey, and roast lamb with cheese, the salad was rich looking with all the vegetables Claire loved, packed in a bucket of ice was a special milky malt whisky brewed in the royal distillery, plus other delicacies that made Claire's tummy to silently rumble for she had eaten nothing all day being so busy with her mother at the market.

At first, Claire thought of not eating but she knew she was going to be sucked and licked by the hungry Duke so there was no point starving herself, so she picked up the golden spoon beside the plate and dug into her buffet, at least if she was going to be sucked and stroked, she better have strength for it. The Duke was pleased to see her eating and started a conversation, he questioned her about her family and was glad to hear that her father was one of his sixty - four gardeners. It impressed him too that Claire had good manners and a graceful posture, just everything he wanted in a queen. Maybe the Lords of the empire will get one of their requests. Gastard thought to himself, yea, the grandest Duke on earth was going to get married he decided, smiling affectionately at Claire.

"Have you ever thought of being queen?" he asked Claire. That question stunned her, she paused her eating for several seconds,

"I'm just a poor girl, your Highness, I dare not dream of offices beyond my reach," Claire carefully answered.

Gastard was very pleased with her humility, she was pleasing him all around without knowing it. He decided there and then that he was going to walk her down the chapel of Zazu empire, the same chapel where his parents were wedded, the sentiments in his head excited him so much that he reached under the table and pinched Claire's nipples so that his chefs wouldn't see, Claire was embarrassed at his moves but kept a straight face since they weren't alone. She didn't know what he was thinking, if she had known he planned to make her queen maybe she would have run for her dear life. Immediately the meal ended, Gastard ordered his servants to bathe Claire in a scented pool, he intended to suck and lick every part of her body and couldn't wait to begin. He already had an erection, a dangerous hard erection that was mercifully hidden under the table. Claire against her wish was taken to the pool and given a thorough bath, the pool smelt of roses, when she emerged, she could smell the most sensational fragrances oozing from her skin, one of the servants, a matronly lady clothed her in a floral robe made of the finest quality with gold embroidery at the edges. Her feet were cushioned with soft Moroccan leather slippers, soft and very attractive. Palace beauticians surrounded her and combed her wavy blonde hair until it sparkled with the hair ointment they applied on it. When a mirror with a gold handle was bought for her, she could hardly recognize herself, her beauty bloomed like never before and she thought herself a goddess. Sitting in his bed-chamber, Gastard was impatient and ordered that Claire be brought immediately. Within seconds, she was ushered in, the transformation he saw in her rendered him speechless, his erection grew longer than ever before, thankfully the servants had exited the chamber, unfortunate Winthrop was given the task of standing outside the door, as usual, to ensure no one bothered the Duke. When they were alone, Gastard within half a second cast off his robe revealing the long full length of him, Claire gasped with fright for she had known no man and wasn't interested in any man. Gastard saw the fright in her eyes and approached her gently, his erection preceding him, Claire closed her eyes as he approached, she could feel his hand in her hair, gently massaging her skull. His hand in her body was repulsive to her yet the sensation he created was terribly sweet, as sweet as chocolate, his erection was touching her at different parts of her body, teasing her skin and feeling her up, very gently he eased her robe off her shoulder, the skin beneath was irresistible so Gastard bent low and kissed her collar bones, he moved to her red sensual lips, Claire tried to struggle free but he clasped her to himself with savage strength and sucked her lips till she saw stars, from her lips he moved to her dreamy eyes and then to her ears, that was too much for Claire so she leaned into his arms, completely overwhelmed by the seduction of the moment. With Claire in his arms, it was a dream come true for him, the most sensual dream of his life was in his arms so he decided to seize his moment. He very gently removed completely the robe on her body and beheld the fullness of her chest, her pink rosy nipples, and the fresh moist triangle between her legs.

CHAPTER FOUR

5. Her hips rose to meet his

Together they shared a breathtaking kiss

The sweetest thing is

His thrusts were strong and firm as trees

10. Hold me for I'm coming

Why do you keep thrusting?

The moistness of the triangle sitting between her legs made him harder, no woman had ever made Gastard that hard or moved him so immensely. He was ready to bow before her and lick her foot, he was ready to be her slave forever if it would buy him just a moment with her in bed. He would divide his kingdom into four, leaving her three portions if she would spread those legs for him, the light curls on her honey pot moved him immeasurably, he wanted to run his fingers through those curls and dig his fingers into her. He wanted to love her to the moon and back, Claire saw the look on Gastard's face and knew she was in trouble. He lifted her off her feet and carried her to his decorated king-sized bed.

Claire commenced struggling again, kicking wildly in his arms, the moment she dreaded all her life had arrived so she fought, hitting him with her dainty palms, her struggles only amused Gastard, he found her kicks sexually provocative and very funny indeed. Before Claire could say, Jack, her back was on the Duke's bed, her eyes widened in shock. Gastard bent over and swept his eyes over her perfect body, very gently he kissed her lips, it tasted like ripe cherries, so he savored it and kissed her deeply and thoroughly, from her lips he moved to her throat line, somehow it tasted like tangerine, Gastard went crazy, he attacked her nipples, pressing gently the roundness of her full breasts, her breasts tasted like pineapples, Gastard had never been with a damsel who tasted so fruity, his eyes sparkled with intense enjoyment and he swore to have her forever. As he sucked hard on her nipples Claire's kicks and struggles reduced, she was beginning to moan and lose her senses, nothing in her entire life prepared her for the sensual ritual on her body meanwhile Gastard sucked on like a hungry child, from her nipples he traced down her stomach line with his tongue, tickling her tender skin and setting her senses on fire, when he got to her navel he sucked hard and Claire screamed with abandon. Winthrop heard her scream and painfully held his erection. When Gastard noticed Claire couldn't more enjoyment on her navel, he moved down to her honey pot but first, he made an announcement

"Claire darling, I'm going to take you to a place you've never been, just spread your legs."

Claire heard his announcement but said nothing, she had no words for him. Very solemnly he slid a long finger into her because she was so tight he stroked her gently, as Claire moaned Winthrop's erection grew painfully harder, his Duke was enjoying himself without thinking of poor Winthrop. Standing right outside the door, Winthrop heard Claire's moan grow louder and decided that he would rather die than stand any further torture, he tiptoed out of his duty post and ran down to the servant's quarters, he needed to find Annie or die. His Annie was at the servants quarters but was busy with another man, when Winthrop peeped into her room through the window, he was shocked to find Bruno another guard in the castle on top of Annie, that disappointment was too much for Winthrop so he banged angrily on the window, for several seconds the two lovers were too carried away to notice him, he banged harder on the window until Bruno condescended to notice him, to Winthrop's shock, Bruno just stood up, went to the window and angrily shut it while Annie roared with laughter. And so unfortunate Winthrop stood there at the servant's quarters, holding his erection and shedding silent tears. Meanwhile, Gastard's tongue was in the honey pot of his sweetheart Claire, she tasted like oranges down there and Gastard loved oranges dearly. Claire kept drifting into paradise and back, she had never felt such sensations, had never dreamt of it, never knew a man could make a woman feel so, it was an experience of a lifetime. When Gastard had sucked enough, he stroked his very erect length and gently spread Claire's legs, the pinkness of her honey pot was a beautiful welcome to his erection, very carefully he started inserting himself into her, he could hear Claire gasping with delight and shock, he continued until he felt a slight blockade, yes she was a virgin just as expected. At first, he paused, then with one swift stroke he entered her completely and Claire screamed. Her scream continued for a few more seconds until her honey pot started sending pleasure waves to all the veins and arteries in her body and brain, she clung to Gastard and he started pounding her, gently at first and when the waves of passion seized him he went harder, on and on they pounded while downstairs Winthrop wept. Suddenly Claire screamed, she had just entered cloud nine for the first time in her life, within seconds Gastard hit cloud nine too and gave one final pound before collapsing on his darling, then something strange happened, as he tried to cuddle Claire, she burst into tears.

CHAPTER FIVE

5. Without permission he stroked me

Forcing my body to see

The pleasures of the room till I agree

That fire flows through my veins hot and free

10. A meeting of naked bodies

Unbridled passion, a sexual treatise

For several minutes Claire wept, tears cascading down her beautiful face and running down her breast mound, Gastard watched her shocked, it had never happened before, all his life no woman had ever wept after tasting his magic touch, her tears was something new and it touched the deepest crevices of Gastard's heart for he was in love, the jerk had fallen in love, for the first time he felt no urge to order her out of bed though she was wailing and wouldn't stop, on the contrary, he wanted to wrap her into his arms and love her. He could hardly believe how he was feeling towards the petite blonde in his arms. When the tears showed no sign of stopping, Gastard became desperate, he promised her half of the gold in Zazu if she would tell what bothered her, he swore to give her the lion share of the vast lands belonging to the Gastard dynasty, he swore never to touch another woman in his life if only she stop the tears for it was breaking his heart just when he discovered he had a heart. Before he met with Claire, he had thought he was an unfeeling emperor who would never fall for someone as fragile as a woman, he had planned to disvirgin all virgins in Zazu and extend his adventures to the nearest kingdoms until he tastes all women and their honey pots sucked all rosy breasts in all their sizes and pumped his seed into every pretty leg spread for him. But with Claire in the picture, he was beginning to feel human warmth for the first time in his miserable life, the thirst to sleep with all virgins was fading away, he found himself wanting only the damsel in his arms and knew he was in mighty trouble, the legend had fallen, the chairman of all fuckaholics was in love. For Claire, it was a different story, her tears were fuelled by different reasons, she just lost her pride to not just a man but to one of the most loathed men in the world, to make matters worse, she enjoyed it, how could she have enjoyed his ruthless erection in her sacred honey pot she asked herself. All her life, she never wanted anything to do with a man, as a child she fancied and stuck with only her female friends, as a teenager, her first love was a chubby girl with red hair. That's pretty shocking, right? A girl? But there it was, Claire's heart was pulled towards the female gender. Incredible but there it was. She remembered her first make-out when she and her childhood friend went to an overgrown garden and pulled at each other's breast while giggling excitedly, for the sensations their tiny breasts gave them tickled them greatly. Crouched inside that garden, they examined each other's vagina and touched their tiny clitoris, shivering with delight and holding each other as they shook with the sensations they created. The memory of this childhood adventure made her cry harder, for the friend was dead and there she was lying in bed with a man who had taken her maidenhead, she and her dead friend had promised each other never to follow any man to his bed, they had promised solemnly to be true to their nature no matter what the world says. They were attracted to fellow damsels and they had no apologies for the world. Gastard, unaware of the conflict in her head, tried to hold her closer but she fought him off.

"Claire darling, do you cry because you think I'll discard you as i did to the others, no my darling, the empire has always wanted a queen and you are queenship personified," Gastard said tenderly to Claire, hoping it would put an end to the river flowing down her eyes, for he meant every word of what he said but Claire was unimpressed.

When she was fifteen, her maternal Aunt married across the western sea and into a royal family visited her parents in Zazu, all dressed in her royal finery. Her Aunt's message was simple, the crown prince of Ameria kingdom, the greatest kingdom across the western sea wanted Claire's hand in marriage, Claire's family were naturally overjoyed and were shocked when Claire said she wasn't interested, her parents had taken her to see a physician for medical examination thinking she was crazy but she stood her ground and after rejecting the Ameria crown prince severally, the suitor was forced to salvage his stung pride and look elsewhere. That was a few years ago, the whole of Zazu had sizzled at the news, for it was unthinkable that a young damsel from an average family would reject opulent royalty. When Claire's father asked her why she refused the Ameria prince, she blurted out that she would have preferred the Ameria princess and not the crowned prince. Her father had held his heart painfully, wondering if he heard right, to prevent him from having a heart attack Claire said it was all a joke and her father exhaled in relief. Deep down her heart, she knew she would rather let a plain princess suck her honey pot than allow the most handsome of princes. The seduction of Gastard took her to the peak of pleasures but that didn't change the nature of her heart and soul. For over an hour she wept until sleep overtook her.

By evening she awoke and found herself alone in the Duke's private chamber but she could hear voices raised in laughter downstairs and glasses clinking together, perhaps some persons were feasting and having a toast. The Duke covered her with a soft thick Egyptian blanket before heading downstairs but underneath the blanket, she was stark naked and she needed a bath for she was covered with the natural juices that come from lovemaking, it wasn't just her body juice, Gastard as he climaxed spread his thick juice liberally on her body, there was sperm on her breast, navel and plenty of it on her vagina. She tiredly rose from the bed and went straight to the bathroom, there was already a steamy scented bath waiting for her, she could see fresh roses in the bath tube, she realized that Gastard had ordered that a bath be prepared for her while she slept. She stepped into the golden bath tube and soaked herself in its refreshing warmth, she had barely started bathing before a uniformed maid knocked and entered, very timidly the maid told Claire that she was instructed by the Duke to give her a bath whenever she woke. Claire was surprised, she never knew royalty involved being waited on hand and foot.

"So how did you know I'm in the bathroom?" Claire asked the maid.

"I've been waiting in the hallway since the Duke went downstairs," the maid explained.

Her name was May, she looked timid and Claire knew the maid would be punished if she failed to do as the Duke instructed, so she let May bathe her. Within seconds, Claire knew that May wasn't as timid as she looked, her hands on Claire's body were bold. May just like Claire loved only women and beautiful women like Claire were her greatest weakness, she massaged Claire's shoulders with a soft sponge and fragrant soap and gently moved down to her breasts, sponging it gently and cunningly brushing Claire's nipples until they tickled. For some unknown reasons, May's indirect seduction pleased Claire more than the vibrant thrusts of Gastard's erection, she closed her eyes and allowed May to scrub her mouth-watering body. Claire's honey pot was filled with Gastard's release so May needed to wash there, that was May's favorite spot, of all the chores she performed in the royal castle that day, the task of washing Claire's body was her favorite, she wished she would be given the task every day. Very gently, May inserted her fingers into Claire's honey pot, as she did that her fingers brushed Claire's clitoris while pretending to wash it, she rolled her fingers inside the honey pot and looked at Claire to gauge her reaction, when she saw Claire's eyes closed, she became bolder and stroked Claire's honey pot faster, assuring her that her honey pot needed washing, that was very pleasurable to Claire and within seconds her hips were mildly moving. May while massaging Claire's honey pot in the name of a wash said there were plenty of soap suds on Claire's breast and that those needed extra washing, Claire said she could go ahead, so while massaging her juicy spot, May used her soft left palm to rub Claire's breast, an interesting erotic wash it was. They both wished the bath would last all evening but May was instructed to quickly finish the bath and dress, Claire, for dinner for there was an important visitor waiting downstairs. Against her wish, May finished the bath and while dressing Claire gazed hungrily at her naked delicious body. Afterward, Claire was taken to the dining hall where the Duke was happily entertaining a tall graceful woman, who looked like royalty. The woman's beauty was eye-catching and pronounced, her poise was graceful and as Claire stepped in, she stared with her mouth open. The Duke was proud to introduce Claire to the woman as her queen to be while the woman was introduced as Gastard's Aunt, her name was Aunt Marvy. Claire was surprised because she never knew the late Duke had a sister, but as she sat down to eat, Gastard told her the full story.

"A lot of people in Zazu don't know I have an Aunt and that's because love took her to a faraway kingdom when I was a little boy. My late parents and many Zazu people didn't understand the love my Aunt found. You see, a rich female merchant once visited Zazu with the golden robes she planned to sell, Aunt Marvy coincidentally visited the market that same day, they both met and it was love at first sight. From that day, Aunt Marvy decided to follow this merchant against the will of my father, that was why she never visited while my parents lived because their relationship cooled afterward. My parents wanted her to marry lord Killigram, a rich landowner in Zazu here, of course, everyone knows lord Killigram but Aunt Marvy made a different choice. Though my parents and Aunt Marvy frequently wrote letters to each other but my Aunt thought it best to stay away or maybe her lover didn't let her, fearing she wouldn't be allowed to return."

At that juncture in Gastard's story, they all laughed, Aunt Marvy blushed when Gastard talked about her lover, Claire realized that Gastard's Aunt was like her, they adored the womenfolk. She could feel Aunt Marvy's eyes on her whenever Gastard wasn't looking. They were eating delicious soup cooked with ham and an assortment of meat, the champagne on the table was chilled and very inviting.

"Tell us about your lover, Aunt Marvy," Claire asked. To their surprise, the question brought tears to Aunt Marvy's eyes.

"That's exactly what I came to tell Gastard," she said, "My lover died two summers ago, she had a fever and never recovered".

They were both sorry for her. Gastard assured Aunt Claire she could stay in the castle as long as she wished.

"It's your home Aunt Marvy. Please feel free to stay till whenever you please," Gastard assured her.

That moment, a pretty maid brought a jar of fresh mango juice, served in an ice bucket, as she turned to leave, Gastard pinched her arse while Claire gasped with shock while Aunt Marvy roared with laughter.

"I've always known Gastard to be a pervert, Claire darling, don't let it bother you," Aunt Marvy said.

Claire wasn't bothered but she was surprised that a man who swore to love her alone some hours ago was pinching another girl's arse right in her presence. Yea, Gastard loved Claire and planned to make her queen but he couldn't stop himself, he loved pretty damsels and wasn't going to apologize for it. To him, women are for two things; for energetic lovemaking and for producing babies. Gastard didn't see why a man shouldn't taste as many women as possible. A man only needs to find the one he loves and make her his wife so she would bear his children while he swims in the ocean of honey pots outside his marriage. That was Gastard's philosophy, so while Claire expected him to apologize he simply winked at her and blew her a kiss. That made Aunt may laugh louder, even the chefs waiting on them at the table had smiles on their faces but they were careful not to let Gastard catch them smiling, he would have given them a knock each on their heads for laughing at jokes meant for royalty. Claire became even more convinced that Gastard was the jerk of the century, she made up her mind never to marry him and bear his name even if it meant being his prisoner forever. She knew Gastard was never going to let her go and nobody could save her but she firmly resolved never to give him the pleasure of being his wife. That night as the clock struck the midnight hour, the whole royal castle was awakened by the most terrifying sound they had ever heard, the beast that terrorized the whole Zazu empire, was roaring right inside the royal castle, it had never happened before. The Duke's castle was a haven that no terror penetrated, yet before their very eyes, they saw the huge she-wolf with blazing red eyes howling in the Duke's courtyard. The knights who kept watch in the Duke's castle picked their swords and fought the beast bravely, one knight was killed in the fight. While they battled, Claire who was asleep in Gastard's arms woke up and stared at the fight downstairs from the window overlooking the courtyard, her eyes grew round with shock, she had never seen such a creature in her life. While she stared, Gastard came from behind and carried her away from the window, he instructed her to stay beneath the covers. Gastard dressed hurriedly and hurried downstairs, he wasn't going to combat the beast Nah never, he was going to firmly lock all the doors and windows leading into the castle, he didn't want to die, who would love all the women in the world if he dies, so he quickly fastened the doors and tried to calm Aunt Marvy who was shivering with fear in the great opulent royal sitting room. Upstairs in the Duke's bed-chamber, Claire was at the window again, the battle downstairs drew her when she should have been afraid, then something strange happened. The beast turned and stared directly at her eyeball to eyeball, Claire jumped away from the window in fright, at that same instant, the beast scaled the castle walls and disappeared into the night.

CHAPTER SIX

5. Two naked bodies meet as one

Breathing in passion, eager to come

Loving and wanting each other more

Two women having a taste of raw passion

10. They drank honey from below their navel

Creating a sensual spark that makes one marvel

There was May and there was Aunt Marvy, right there on the grand bed in the royal castle, there in that room where Aunt May lived as a girl several years ago, they were entwined like two ropes on that grand bed, Aunt Marvy found the maid's body young, firm and beautiful, the mound of May's honey pot was big, fresh and moist. Aunt Marvy dipped two fingers at once into May's honey pot, when she removed those fingers, they were coated with the bright juice of May's honey pot. May found Aunt Marvy to be a professional lover and relaxed, giving up her body to the sensual touch of the century. With May relaxed, Aunt Marvy took over and started to do what she knew how to do best, she spread May's legs so wide that each leg was almost at the edge of the massive bed. She bent low and put her soft lips to May's honey pot, she sucked her clitoris until May screamed with uncontrolled delight. As May screamed, Aunt Marvy sucked harder, dipping her tongue into the soft folds of May's vagina, May's eyes rolled up, showing only the whites of her eyes for she was in another world. Still doing wonders at May's honey pot, Aunt Marvy used her left palm to cup the very firm breast of May, massaging her nipples mercilessly, she did this for several minutes tirelessly while May nearly flew out of her body with ecstasy. As May gasped, Aunt Marvy increased the number of fingers in May's honey pot to four, she started stroking the young damsel faster and stronger until May climaxed violently.

For several seconds, May's body floated in space, she didn't know where she was, all she felt was the hot sweet sensation in between her legs. When she eventually floated into her body, Aunt Marvy was ready to receive what she had given May. With Aunt Marvy's tall athletic body spread on the massive bed, May with the agility of youth pounced in me. Aunt Marvy's body was perfectly toned, it was difficult to believe she was forty for she looked fifteen years younger. Her breasts were as large as watermelons yet it was firm and tantalizing with pink nipples that looked inviting and incredibly seductive. May was hungry for the Sweetness Aunty Marvy had to offer and Aunt Marvy gave her body up for pleasure.

It all started the morning after Aunt Marvy arrived at the royal castle, after the attack on the castle by the beast. That morning, Aunt Marvy came out to have breakfast with Gastard and Claire when May and other maids came to wait on the diners, Aunt Marvy set her eyes on May and swore to herself that she was going to fuck her. While the maids were serving them breakfast, Aunt Marvy requested that May bring her a jar of fresh milk, as May brought the jar close, Aunt May put her hands under the table and rubbed May's thighs, May was pleasantly surprised and smiled shyly at Aunt Marvy. Gastard saw their moves but didn't care, he loved sex and didn't see why others shouldn't enjoy themselves, he wished them well in their sexual exploit, only Claire didn't know what was going on, she didn't care anyway, for her mind was occupied with her imprisonment in the Duke's castle, Gastard made it clear that Claire would never leave the castle until she agreed to marry him. As a matter of fact, after breakfast that morning, Gastard ordered three royal guards led by Gerrard to carry bars of gold, robes of the finest quality, from golden robes to rich velvet and silk robes, assorted edibles of different categories, and wads of money to Claire's family, the guards were instructed to inform Claire's family that she was a prisoner of the Duke and would remain so until she agreed to marry him and bear his children, also they were informed that Claire wasn't allowed to entertain visitors, not even family members, the idea was to pressurize her into marrying the naughty Duke. After breakfast that morning, Aunt Marvy found an excuse to go to the kitchen and whispered into May's ears that she would like to see her in her room by evening. And so that evening, May abandoned all chores by the strict orders of Aunt Marvy and went to the grand room where Aunt Marvy waited stark naked.

CHAPTER SEVEN

5. His erection is seen everywhere

For he's got a sexual flair

That puts him in all ladies legs

His hardness is a randy peg

10. The ladies scream with pleasure

For with his erection he tickles their treasure

A week after the sexual exploitation of May and Aunt Marvy, the Zazu empire experienced another threat of war from king Arthur because Gastard mischievously crossed his boundaries again. Ever since the first day he danced in between Claire's legs, he didn't get another chance because she violently r refused him sex, he couldn't stay without his daily bedroom gymnastics so he went searching for a damsel that suits his taste. He had different maids in his castle who were feminine perfection, with all the qualities a man can ever desire in a lady, he had tasted all of them and wanted something new. To make matters worse, the damsels of Zazu avoided him like a plague when they saw him coming, somebody would whisper fuckaholic and everyone would run. The nearest kingdom was King Arthur's and the maidens in that kingdom were as beautiful as fairies, the very reason Gastard sneaked into princess Morgana's bed some time ago, King Arthur's damsels were not just fairies, they had cherry faces and trim shapes, they were also reputed to be warm, soft and very tender when they are in a room with a man, so Gastard abandoned all the problems in his kingdom, including the daily night attack of the she-wolf on his castle ever since he took Claire as a prisoner of love, he forgot the deadly terror his people suffered when he sneaked into princess Morgana's bed, he forgot all these and went hunting again in King Arthur's kingdom, traveling in his royal entourage. Gastard escorted by his finest knights entered King Arthur's kingdom, he created the impression that he was traveling to Ameria kingdom and therefore needed to pass through king Arthur's territory. He intended to pick out the finest damsels of the land, load them with gifts of gold and then bring them back to his castle in Zazu. He met Clara whose skin was as shiny as the brightness of the morning sun, Clara whose lips were an invitation to a kiss, whose chest had breasts that pointed at men, whose hips were round and inviting, Clara who was sexuality on two legs. On sighting Clara, Gastard's royal carriage pulled to a stop, and Clara who was in the company of her friend Susanna was invited into Gastard's carriage. Clara was very beautiful but hadn't much sense, so when Gastard flattered the perfection of her body, she smiled from ear to ear, her friend Susanna was awed by the wealth written all over Gastard and because she was reasonably beautiful, right there in the royal carriage, Gastard lifted their robes and dipped his fingers into their young vaginas at the same time, the young virgins giggled and blushed with embarrassment as the royal carriage reversed and headed back to Zazu

Gastard ordered his carriage driver to drive faster, to knock down anybody that stood on their way, his erection was strong and he needed to get to his castle and feed on the naive beauties giggling beside him. When they arrived at Zazu, they drove very hurriedly to the castle, flogging the horses and urging them to run faster for Gastard's erection was about exploding. They arrived at the castle and the young girls were taken to Gastard's private chambers, Claire was in the royal garden when Gastard arrived with the two young virgins but she wasn't bothered. She was relieved, because, with the two girls, Gastard will be too satisfied to disturb her sleep at night. Gastard's eyes locked with Claire's as he went in with the girls, he winked at Claire and smiled foolishly. In the privacy of his bed-chamber, Gastard unrobed these two beauties and pounced on them, stroking them simultaneously and squeezing their young breasts like soft oranges. Tirelessly he spread their legs and ate their young vaginas one after the other, with the girls screaming their heads off as he poked around in their young pussies, Winthrop as usual listened painfully at their enjoyment from his post outside the door while silently cursing the Duke. When Gastard finished with the maidens, he was so tired because their youthful strength had sapped him of all energy but he was very happy, he just disvirgined two beauties at the same time and that pleased him mightily. But then the Duke would always be the Duke, for as the girls were chattering on the bed, Gastard rose and ordered them to leave, when Winthrop heard the order from his position at the door, he quickly gathered the bars of gold that would be used to compensate the damsels. The girls were shocked Susanna went as far as crying for Gastard had promised to marry one of them, it was the promise that made her spread her legs, Clara was too angry for words, her anger waa. Such that her skin turned red but Gastard wasn't bothered, he wanted them out of his bed and that was final. The girls laden with assorted bars of gold were driven back to their home and two days later, Gastard received a letter declaring war on Zazu. It turned out that Clara was the daughter of a war general who was called sir Hareton. When sir Hareton heard of his daughter's defilement, he matched angrily to King Arthur's palace and asked for permission to storm Zazu with his knights. King Arthur remembered what Gastard did to Morgana and heartily gave his blessing to Sir Hareton, he had only one wish and that was for Sir Hareton and his knights to bring back Gastard's randy penis souvenir. Two days after Gastard received the threat, King Arthur's knights struck, they attacked all Zazu people who were seen outside the great walls of the Zazu empire. Some survived these attacks and reported back to the Duke while others were killed. A few were taken as prisoners, it dawned on Gastard and the whole of Zazu that what they feared most had happened, they only prayed that king Arthur's sorcerer Merlin, would not be involved in the war, for only a portion of his magic concoction would wipe the whole Zazu. To make matters worse while King Arthur's knights harassed Zazu citizens outside the walls of Zazu during the day, the beast harassed the people inside Zazu walls at night. The people were under severe peril, they battled enemies on two fronts, they also knew it was a matter of time before King Arthur's knight enter Zazu for a full-blown fight, their harassment of people outside Zazu walls was just a taste of what was to come, their way of telling the Duke of Zazu to prepare his knights for battle. When the peoples' cry became too painful to be ignored, the Duke was forced to call a meeting of all the lords and generals. Lord Henry, Gastard's ex-prisoner was there and had something to say, he told Gastard for the second time how he was a disappointment to the Zazu empire for his libido had once again gotten the whole of Zazu into severe trouble. The Duke was too tense by the situation in Zazu to take offense so he allowed lord Henry to get away with his remarks but urged him to find a solution and not cry over spilt milk. Lord Henry in his usual calculated manner, told the royal court to send a peaceful delegate to king Arthur, these delegates were to carry a thousand bars of gold, 500 rubies, and 50 baskets of silver to king Arthur as compensation for the two virgins who were eaten at once by Duke Gastard. The gifts for king Arthur looked massive but it was nothing to the affluent Zazu empire. The delegates led by lord Henry approached King Arthur with humility, though they were harassed but the eloquence and wisdom of lord Henry calmed all boiling tempers especially sir Hareton who wanted Gastard's head. Sir Hareton, whose wife was late, demanded that a virgin from Zazu be given to him as compensation for his daughter Clara who was mercilessly defiled by Zazu's Duke. lord Henry thought of his request and found it reasonable, sir Hareton was very good looking, wealthy, and was above all a courageous knight, qualities many ladies love dearly, he knew loads of Zazu maidens would want to marry sir Hareton and si he and the other delegates returned to Zazu to report to the Duke and find a virgin wife for the enraged sir Hareton. Gastard accepted sir Hareton's terms besides he had more pressing issues bothering him, the beast's attack on his castle was getting fiercer, it bothered him that the beast had started entering his royal castle, a thing never heard of, Gastard knew it all started the very day he forcefully took Claire, he knew it was significant and it worried him sorely, so he quickly accepted sir Hareton's demands and decided that it was time to consult the witch living in the dark Zazu caves.

CHAPTER EIGHT

5. He wanted all women,

For they give pleasure to men

Their body honey to taste and tame

Wondrous beauties a man must claim

10. He loves to put his seed in them

Dancing inside their legs, young and firm

Sir Hareton got his wish, a young Zazu maiden with very pink lips, fresh face, small beautiful eyes, and silky long hair, whose beauty was adequate compensation for sir Hareton, besides she had known no man. Her name was Alicia and she was as fair as a water spirit. When She was taken to sir Hareton by Lord Henry and the other Zazu knights, sir Hareton took one look at her and wanted her. He had feared that he was going to hate whoever lord Henry brought to him because the memory of what the randy Zazu Duke did to his daughter was still very fresh in his memory, but he saw Alicia and knew he had forgiven Gastard and the whole of Zazu. Lord Henry could see that the man in Sir Hareton approved of the beauty brought to him, besides it was easy to see the instant attraction between young Alicia and sir Hareton for sir Hareton offered lord Henry and the knights refreshments, another sign that he loved the damsel he was given. It was obvious to everyone that sir Hareton needed a private moment with his young wife, a man recognizes another man's desire for a woman and so lord Henry rushed his refreshment and urged the knights to do the same. Within a short while they were on their way to Zazu, leaving young Alicia in her new home, the matter was once again settled, they returned to Zazu to combat the terror of the beast which was yet to be settled.

In Zazu, Gastard was begging for a minute with Claire, she was seated on the vast royal bed with her legs crossed and her face stern, the Duke was shamelessly on his knees humbly begging to take the Sweetness inside her legs, when Claire noticed that his erection was getting more dangerous, she started walking away from the royal chamber, leaving Gastard on his knees, that move turned out to be unfortunate for her, for as she walked away, Gastard saw her gently swaying bottom and went crazy, he grabbed her from behind and she screamed, Winthrop always outside the door locked the door from outside, there was no escape for Claire. Gastard pulled up her robe and discovered to his pleasure that she wore nothing underneath for she had her bath a while ago, that was all the chance he needed, holding the petite pretty Claire with his strong left arm, he unbuttoned his pant, flung his robe to the farthest corner of his bedchamber and positioned Claire's honey pot, he entered her with one swift powerful stroke from the back and Claire screamed, he had wanted her for a long time so he explored her honey pot with powerful strokes, when Claire started moaning, he increased the intensity of his strokes and started pounding her young vagina. Lifting her to his knees, he gave it to her like he was possessed and Claire had multiple orgasms. She hated him yes, but who can control the enjoyment and Sweetness of the flesh? After a whole hour, it was all over, Claire lay on the vast bed covering her moist young honey pot with her hands for it was on fire, her breast looked raw for Gastard had sucked them like a hungry baby while pounding her like a mad lover. Gastard planted a kiss on her forehead and hurriedly started dressing, he needed to urgently see the witch in the Zazu dark caves, he needed her help for she understood the hot situation he was into, she had helped him in the times past, he needed her help once more to tame the beast that boldly roamed his castle every night. Just the night before, the beast came as usual at the midnight hour and started howling right beneath Gastard's window, a habit the beast had as if Gastard held a property belonging to it. When the knights attacked the she-wolf, one of them was maimed and the others retreated while the beast scaled the castle walls untouched. And so Gastard entered his golden coach, escorted by five brave knights, he made his way to the witch's cave outside the protective walls of Zazu.

CHAPTER NINE

5. Well, he's frankly a fuckaholic

Worse than an alcoholic

For he loves to screw and frolic

His adventure a tale quite erotic

10. If you are a sexualized esoteric

Then you're a legend, enjoy my topic

On the way to the Zazu caves, Gastard's heart pounded painfully and relentlessly, he was fortunate to be alone in his royal carriage because anyone sitting close to him would have heard the painful fluttering of his heart, the five knights who escorted him were split into two other carriages which formed his royal procession, three knights rode in the first carriage ahead of him while the remaining two rode behind, the idea was to protect the Duke from dangers coming from the front and from behind. Gastard's knights were frankly afraid too, though they were brave warriors, they knew they were going to meet a ruthless witch, an almost savage creature and it unnerved them. The Zazu witch was famed for her ruthlessness yet she was as beautiful as a fallen angel, maybe she was a fallen angel, cast out from heaven due to the vileness of her heart. Her magic wasn't as potent as that of the cele-brated Merlin who gave king Arthur protection yet she was feared for she had the habit of turning her enemies and sometimes innocent people into hideous animals and monsters. She was accused of turning a certain unfortunate but fine-looking young man into a monkey, his offense was that he refused to be her lover and loved another damsel. When the witch discovered this youth's heart wasn't with her, she turned him into an ugly-looking monkey, everyone knew she was responsible for that wickedness, yet no one had the nerves to accuse her to her face for no one wanted to die. There were other cases too of innocent persons she turned into rocks, toads, snakes, whatever she deemed fit. It was widely believed that out of the six caves that form her dwelling, one is a human turned into a cave. She once in a fit of rage turned a man into a huge penis for spying on her while she was having her bath. People wondered how such a mouth-watering beauty managed to have such a wicked terrible heart, she was an object of curiosity for she was an incredible mixture of honey and vinegar, beauty and horror. She was generally known in all the kingdoms as the nameless witch. In less than an hour, Gastard's procession entered the narrow lane leading to the woods which sheltered her dark caves. On getting to the edge of the woods, Gastard and his knights alighted from their carriages for the woods could only be maneuvered by foot. Three knights preceded Gastard as usual while two stayed behind him, protecting him from the wild animals domiciled in the woods. They walked on for several yards in the thickness of the woods until they saw the dark caves, they paused momentarily in fear for they knew the evil that lurked inside those caves, they could see a bright fire burning outside the six caves and human skulls hanging outside the entrance of each if they weren't brave men they would have turned and run back to the safety of Zazu, but they continued, moving more cautiously until they got to the entrance of the cave. Gastard called out to the nameless witch, he called her four consecutive times before she responded and invited them in. They walked in cautiously in a single file, taking care not to match the various bones lying across the stone floor of the cave, their footsteps echoed, instilling fear in their hearts. Though the entrance of the caves was less than five feet tall the inside was vast, with high rocky walls and various rooms. The voice of the witch directed them until they found themselves in a vast room that had a blazing fire in the hearth, *various carvings representing the gods and goddesses of the sea, hills, and other gods the witch served and dedicated her life to. There were also stone seats carved out from the rocks of the cave, it was on these stone seats that Gastard and his knights sat, the witch herself, a very tall figure with curves that could make a man forget her scary priesthood and lay her out on a beautiful bed, she had very dark lashes and a raven black long hair which contrasted beautifully with the whiteness of her skin, her eyes were sharp and searching, her stare was direct and bold, cat-like eyes that missed nothing. She has big full breasts that bounced as she moved. When the Duke and his knights were seated, she stared fixedly at them until they quivered fearfully in their seats when they had given up hope of ever hearing anything from her, she burst out laughing, showing a perfect dentition the Duke and the knights didn't know why she laughed but they smiled politely to avoid annoying her, when Gastard opened his mouth to table his problems, she hushed him for she already knew his problems and she told him so, Gastard wasn't surprised for she was the invisible eye that roamed around Zazu, therefore she knew a lot of things.*

"You know the procedure Duke," she said.

"Before you state your problems, no matter how numerous or weighty they are, you must first pay me handsomely". Gastard smiled mischievously, he knew the payment expected of him, it wasn't cash payment, the witch would never accept monetary payment for her sorcery, she had gold mines that gave her a sea of wealth, so all those who were brave enough to seek her services knew the payment she required.

Because of her magic powers, she hardly saw men, therefore all men that sought her magic had to pay on her bed, her female patronizers paid the same way too for she loved both men and women. Gastard needed no second prompting, for the witch even with all her sorcery looked as delicious as cake and so with a foolish grin on his face, he extended his hands to her and led her to the inner cave. He had visited her before and knew that particular inner cave for he had serviced her on that bed before. The inner cave was surprisingly cozy for that was where the witch satisfied and cooled the hunger and fire in between her legs, there was comfortable and soft bedding at a corner of the cave, the floor wasn't rocky like the rest of the cave but was covered with colorful varieties of animal skin, the witch was a sorceress no doubt but was also a woman and her feminine taste was seen in the decor of her inner cave, the stone window at the far end of the cave had a beautiful silky curtain that kept out the insect noise from the forest. There was a stone wardrobe at another corner of the cave where the witch hung flowing but eye-catching robes of the witch hung, she was wearing one of those long robes as Gastard led her to the bed. She did not wear anything underneath that robe of hers and her arse dangled freely without restraint, so freely that as Gastard led the witch away, the knights stared hungrily at her retreating back, Gerrard who was one of them licked his lips wishing he was the Duke. Gastard laid the witch gently on the bed and removed his robes, then he proceeded to remove hers. On removing her robe, he found out that she was already wet for she hungrily anticipated the big hard erection of the Duke, Gastard was happy to see that she anticipated him, he smiled that foolish smile of his again and placed himself solidly between her long straight legs, the witch's clitoris was big and pink, it was also very wet like it could hardly wait to receive the big hardness of the Duke. Gastard loved round full chests so he put his face on the witch's breast and sucked happily until the witch's hips were bouncing hungrily on the bed, begging for his penetration, when Gastard had sucked his fill, he positioned his big hardness at the entrance of the very wet vagina and plunged in, his penetration was sweet and filling so the witch screamed in ecstasy, the knights cursed her under their breath for as she screamed, they all experienced wild erections and there was no hope of relief. The witch's honey pot was very wet and sugary so Gastard threw caution to the wind and pounded her hard, so hard that the noise of their lovemaking was heard in all the six caves and in the woods, some monkeys were seen swinging on the trees close to the cave, perhaps they were attracted by the wild sex inside the witch's cave and came to see for themselves. The witch was skilled in bedroom affairs, so as Gastard pounded her hard, she raised her hips, matching his thrusts energetically, she gave him and received from him until their eyes shone brightly like fire and suddenly they climaxed at the same time, screaming at the top of their voices, by then, Gastard's knights were already as hard as rocks beneath their robes. Gastard and the witch emerged from the inner cave smiling happily while the knights looked sad. Because Gastard paid very handsomely, the witch gave him listening ears as he poured out his heart and explained his troubles. When he finished, the witch signaled to him that they needed to talk privately, the Duke told his knights they were free to stretch their legs, the knights happily escaped, besides seeing the witch didn't help their erection. When the Duke and the witch were alone, the witch told Gastard that the she-wolf had a very strong spirit, her spirit was as strong as that of her ancestors, the witch explained, the only way to stop the wolf from entering the castle was to bury the hidden bottle containing the hair of the beast. Gastard understood completely because some time ago, he and the witch under the cover of darkness at the midnight hour turned a lovely creature into a she-wolf using the powers of the nameless witch, a magical spell that permanently turned the lovely creature into a beast that prowled at the midnight hour, a condition that was meant to remain forever unless the wolf's hair which was bottled and hidden in the royal castle was broken by one who loves the beast. To Gerrard and the nameless witch, no human on the surface of the earth would ever love a beast, a she-wolf with long claws and sharp canine that tears human flesh, the she-wolf was fated to walk the earth until the hour of her death. The witch so enjoyed the Duke's love-making that she decided to follow him back to his castle and bury the bottle. Gastard was excited, he could see his troubles coming to an end, very quickly the witch packed her leather bag containing her magic portions and followed the Duke. Together, the Duke, witch, and knights all walked through the woods and entered the royal carriage.

The witch's presence in the royal castle caused quite a stir, all the persons that lived in that great castle scurried away from her like rats, nobody wanted to be turned into an insect, rodent, or anything that pleased the nameless witch. She was an esteemed guest despite her sorcery and so the chefs of the royal family were ordered to slaughter a ram and prepare a feast, meanwhile, the Duke descended into the basement where the royal family stored the best of wines and priceless whiskeys in a magnificent cellar, the Duke personally picked some bottles of wine for the witch and within seconds, those bottles of wine were being chilled in a bucket of ice. The Duke made the witch comfortable in his vast magnificent sitting room and shortly they were relaxing with the chilled bottles of wine, they weren't in a hurry because their task was to be done at midnight. When the meal was ready, the roast lamb and the rich salad were laid out in the dining hall, there was an assortment of fresh fruits to serve as a desert; pineapples, apples, grapes, blueberries, and other fruits chefs could lay their hands on. Aunt Marvy and Claire joined the Duke and the witch at the dining hall, the witch on sighting Claire eyed her with interest so Gastard told her that Claire was his, the future queen of Zazu, that checked the interest of the witch but didn't completely stop her from eyeing Claire when the Duke wasn't looking. The chefs served the. meal and all at the table attacked the sumptuous food. Making conversations at the table was a bit difficult because both Aunt Marvy and Claire feared the witch, they weren't completely at ease in her presence. The meal was about finishing when a maid brought in fresh hand towels for the diners and screamed on seeing the witch, the maid knew the witch for when she was little, the witch turned her half brother into a frog, the poor maid kept screaming with fright until the witch got angry and was about turning her into a snail when the Duke pleaded on behalf of his maid. The frightened maid was taken away and the atmosphere relaxed. After the meal, Aunt Marvy hurriedly left the table for she was very uncomfortable around the witch, Claire too found an excuse to leave, she was going upstairs when on second thought she decided to eavesdrop on the conversation of the Duke and the witch, it puzzled her that the Duke was foolish enough to consort with a creature as wicked as the witch, so she decided to risk the witch's wrath and listen to her conversation with the Duke behind the walls of the dining hall. It turned out that Claire's brave decision became a turning point in the lives of so many innocent people and a turning point for the Zazu empire as a whole. Claire listened carefully and overheard the witch telling the Duke that the bottle would need to be buried deep into the earth so that the she-wolf would never take her human form again. Claire's heartbeat with fear at what she heard, dawned on her that the she-wolf wasn't originally a beast but was an unfortunate human who was caged in the body of a beast through the witch's wicked sorcery. She was tempted to run to the safety of the Duke's cozy rooms lest the witch turn her into something worse than a she-wolf but she realized that the destiny of the poor creature wasting in a beast's body could be helped by her. It occurred to her that maybe fate allowed her to overhear the conversation so she would help, so with her heart beating fearfully and her legs shaking she continued listening until she heard when the witch asked Gastard if the bottle was still under his bed and if he was sure that he was ready to bury the bottle forever. Claire had heard enough, she quickly fled upstairs and lying flat on the floor searched under the bed and found a green bottle locked securely with an evil looking rag, inside the bottle was a human hair, Claire's hand shook terribly as she reached for the bottle, she felt courage running through her veins, despite her fear, like she was created to save the poor beast, she grabbed the bottle firmly but a question arose in her mind on what to do with it. She didn't yet know the nooks and crannies of the vast castle with its numerous rooms, besides servants, butlers, and various domestic staff were randomly at various corners of the castle, so she could bump into any of them while trying to hide the bottle. Well, there was the need to hide the bottle and quickly too no matter what, so she put the bottle under her robe and boldly marched out of the Duke's bed-chamber. Winthrop was as usual seated across the door for it was his duty to prevent anyone aside from the Duke and Claire from entering the Duke's private chamber. Claire didn't know where to put the bottle, but she was determined to stroll casually around the castle until she found a perfect spot. She found servants doing several chores at different corners of the castle so she strolled out of the castle and directed her steps towards the royal garden. As a child, she and her little friends took pleasure in hiding things where no adult could find them, the memory brought a smile to Claire's face, servants that passed her that moment wondered what tickled the Duke's love but Claire hardly saw them, she was intently preoccupied with what she was going to do to thwart the wicked plans of the Duke and the nameless witch. Her heartbeat very loudly, it was a wonder that no one heard the wild fearful beating of her heart, she strolled casually into the garden and when she was cer-

tain that no one was watching, she hid the bottle in between the thick bush of cherries, so artfully was the bottle hidden that no one but Claire could easily find it. Having accomplished her task, Claire strolled out and headed towards the horse stables to complete the impression that she was taking a stroll within the castle environs. When she re-entered the castle, the Duke and the witch were still busy with their vile conversation but Claire couldn't eavesdrop further because a servant was at that moment doing a task nearby. She climbed upstairs to scan underneath the bed a second time just in case more frightful things were there. She had made love with Gastard severally on that bed without knowing that a life was bottled beneath, her scan revealed nothing out of ordinary, so she lay on the bed happy that she had done something useful before Claire knew it, sleep overtook her and she had a strange dream, in that dream she saw this ;

Every night a she-wolf prowled a graceful beast, slashing the night air with her long bushy tail like a gifted swordsman slicing through the invisible air with his sword. The girl could see the beast's lean hairy but oddly seductive flanks as she growled, her paws taping the royal castle grounds in an even pattern, when the beast flashed her coal red eyes at the girl and let out a howl, the whole castle covered with fear but sitting in the castle garden the girl stretched out her hands to the beast without fear for they were lovers, woman, and beast, an unprecedented love soiree, can you beat that? But that's the love they found, you shall soon understand when you hear my story, meanwhile, the wolf howled her way towards the girl, stepped daintily over the garden flowers, and stood firmly before the girl stopped her blood-curdling howl. For several seconds the beast considered the girl's outstretched hands, the girl watched the wolf's face relax into a beastly smile, without much ado the beast stepped into the girl's arms and started to whimper in the enjoyment of the moment and because of the gruesome pain she daily had to suffer, the girl gently fingered the soft furs of the beast and closed her eyes with a mixture of mild fear and anticipated Sweetness as the beast opened her Jaws, revealed her gleaming teeth and took the girl's white tender breast into her great Jaws, the girl collapsed into the roses, enjoying the moment.

Then Claire awoke, she was covered with sweat for she realized she was the girl in the dream mating with the she-wolf but then something was turning in her memory, the eyes of the she-wolf though blood-red looked like and reminded her of the eyes of her childhood friend who died some time ago, the same friend she had her first make out with inside an overgrown garden. Those eyes were indeed the eyes of that friend, it was very strange and so scary but she missed her friend and decided she was going to hide in the royal garden and observe the beast more closely, she couldn't explain it but she felt drawn towards that beast, a strong pull she couldn't explain, it was like fate pulling her towards her destiny. As a child, Claire was spanked with a small cane that was her size for always going on daring, dangerous, childish, adventures. That daring spirit remained with her and she resolved finally that she going to be at the royal garden

CHAPTER TEN

5. Love is love

Whether it's a man or woman, there's love to give

And plenty of cuddles to receive

10. There's love to be made

Sweet pleasure, sharp as a blade.

As the day grew darker, Gastard told Claire that he would like her to sleep in a big comfortable room downstairs as he and the witch had an important ritual to perform in his bed-chamber, he told Claire that the ritual was for the progress of the whole empire, Claire pretended to believe him and obediently went downstairs as he said. The servants were surprised that no one was allowed to go near the numerous rooms in the upper part of the castle. The reason was simple, Gastard didn't want anyone to overhear the details of the ritual he and the witch were going to perform. Minutes to the midnight hour, Claire stole out of her room and bravely sneaked into the garden, spread a thick blanket on the floor behind a high flower hedge and sat behind it, waiting for the beast.

There was absolute stillness in the castle, all servants had gone to sleep, only the knights on patrol stayed awake, they knew the beast was going to strike as usual so the knights on patrol were vigilant, waiting for the beast to appear so they would alert other knights. As the huge castle clock struck the midnight hour, right at that second, Claire felt the hairs on her body stand, she didn't need to be told that there was magic in the air, she felt her spirit being pulled by an unseen force, fear-filled her heart and she thought of running inside the comfort of her bedroom but before she could do that, there was an alarm from the knights, the she-wolf was spotted on the wall of the castle, the knights who were sleeping were instantly on their feet, in unison they drew their swords and formed a battle-ready defensive position, the beast like a classy lady ignored them as if they were naughty children and walked right towards the garden. Claire's eyes grew round in terror as the beast approached her steadily as if they were on a date, Claire prayed silently that the beast would change direction, but it was like it perceived Claire's body fragrance and would not change direction. Claire closed her eyes tightly until she felt a presence before her, a powerful presence, so she opened her eyes and beheld in very close quarters the she-wolf that terrorized the whole Zazu empire. Claire looked into its red hot eyes and quietly fainted. The knights saw the beast walking into the vast royal garden and were surprised because the beast always howled beneath the Duke's window. Anyway, for the knights, the beast walking into the garden which was a bit distant from the castle saved them the problem of fighting and putting their lives on the line. Meanwhile, the witch and Gastard were in Gastard's bed-chamber, the witch set her magic portions strategically, she told Gastard to bring out the green bottle so she would chant her magic lines and seal the spirit of the she-wolf with the spirit of the helpless human living inside the wolf together forever. Gastard nodded and reached under the bed for the bottle but got the shock of his life, the bottle was missing, he alone knew about the bottle, he was in trouble, the spirits the witch served told him if the bottle wasn't buried, then events would take an ugly turn against him, they Warned him and now the bottle was missing, worse still he couldn't ask any of his numerous servants since no one was there when the bottle was given to him, he and the witch were alone when the lovely creature was turned to a she-wolf. Yet the bottle was missing, the witch's face turned scary with anger, her magic powers were burning hot and ready to be used yet the Duke was telling stories. The Duke suddenly started sweating, his latest problem was too much for him, how could his world so crash around him yet he couldn't run to anyone for help, while the Duke tried to sort out himself, Claire in the royal garden was recovering from her faint but as she came back to her senses, she realized she was lying on something furry and hairy, when her senses were completely clear, she opened her eyes and beheld the face of the beast looking down directly at her, she would have fainted again except that the beast's eyes looked very much familiar, so arrestingly familiar like never before. It was no longer red hot and angry looking but looked exactly like a human eye, exactly or almost exactly like the eyes of her childhood friend, to make matters more confusing, the face of the she-wolf was relaxing into a beastly smile, Claire was supposed to be terrified but she found herself smiling back at the beast, it was then it occurred to her that she was lying on the hairy legs of the beast, the beast must have protectively cushioned her head when she fainted, that made Claire feel safe around the beast, okay to be frank, she didn't feel altogether safe but she suspected the beasts wasn't going to hurt her. As the she-wolf's face remained fixed in a smile, Claire relaxed, she felt her heart being pulled towards the she-wolf everyone hated and feared, her heart warmed to the beast just the way it warmed her best friend before death separated them. A beast that killed knights and fought everyone took care of her when she fainted so Claire decided that the she-wolf wanted her friendship and because the beast's eye looked like her best friend's, Claire decided that she was going to befriend the beast. She discovered that while the beast stayed with her, it stayed calm and made no attempt to hurt anybody, so Claire thinking smartly as always decided that she was going to always keep the beast busy every midnight, that way, nobody gets hurt. Besides, the she-wolf that held her protectively was friendly and she found herself returning the beast's friendship.

CHAPTER ELEVEN

5. He saw a fresh vagina

Asking for his sexual stamina

Yet he appeared naive like a foreigner

For his life was threatened by a harbinger

10. If body delights were life

He would screw his life out of strife

"Spread your legs wide Annie," Winthrop said to Annie, the royal kitchen maid who was very kind with her honey pot, she was beloved of most of the men in the royal castle for she let them take turns pounding her young horny honey pot.

That fateful night, it was Winthrop's turn, the same night Claire found a strange friendship with the she-wolf and Gastard sweated uncontrollably for he had lost the locked green bottle, it was that same night that Winthrop got Annie to himself for it was finally his turn and he didn't see why he shouldn't make himself happy, after all the Duke always had his pleasures without thinking of the problems of other people, without thinking also of the hard erection poor Winthrop suffered as he stood on guard outside his bed-chamber while the Duke for whom he suffered enjoyed himself with countless young virgins, so Winthrop seized his moment, he had suffered painful unreleased erections for too long and so when he took Annie to his bed that night, he used his fingers to spread wide her pink honey pot and sucked her clitoris mercilessly until Annie's leg started shaking. When she couldn't take more sucking there, Winthrop moved to her breast, he sucked and gave her young breasts sweet love bites and when his erection became as hard as iron, he spread her legs wide and rammed his full hard length right into her steamy honey pot. Annie closed her eyes in ecstasy and raised her hips, taking in the full hard length of him, her honey pot swallowed the full length of him completely. Winthrop positioned himself carefully on the bed and started hitting her honey pot like he was crazy, Annie was very experienced in love affairs, especially bedroom affairs, so she raised her hips repeatedly to meet his wild thrusts, they sweated together though the weather was very cold, for they were creating heat through the frenzy and intensity of their entanglement. When Winthrop couldn't contain the Sweetness of Annie's honey pot, he raised her gently and took her to another position, and before Annie could adjust properly in the new position, Winthrop was already pounding her hard so she concentrated on moaning, for the sweet sensation running through her young body started from her honey pot and spread through her veins and straight to her brain. Of all her lovers in the royal castle, Winthrop was the second-best in pounding her ever-horny honey pot. The best was the Duke, yea the Duke who couldn't say no to a moist honey pot. When Annie started working for the Duke, within twenty- four hours, she could feel the eyes of the great Zazu Duke on her young body as she served his meals and ran errands for him. Within the same twenty-four hours, the Duke sneaked his palms into her skirt and brushed the tips of her vagina, making her blush bright pink for she was then a Virgin. When in the evening the Duke requested for a bottle of whiskey to be brought to his private chambers, Annie took the desired whiskey and while she served it, the Duke reached boldly into her evening dress and brought out her young soft breasts, pressing them gently. Annie had covered her face with her palms because the Duke's actions embarrassed her but the Duke carried her to his grand bed, removed her clothes, and spread her legs when he touched and rolled the tips of his hardness on her young honey pot, Annie went to paradise and returned. By the time the Duke gently drove his hardness into her moist sweet pleasure spot, she knew she was going to love sex forever. So to Annie, the Duke was the first and best, followed immediately by Winthrop who was pounding her young pussy with vengeance. Winthrop once again took her to another position, this time around he kept her on her knees on the floor of the room and rammed his rock hard length into her from behind, for several minutes, he took her to the world of pleasure in that position, Annie's scream was heard in several rooms, disturbing the peace of innocent occupants of those rooms, when her scream became too piercing and shrill, Gerrard whose room was not too far away marched angrily to Winthrop's room and banged repeatedly on the door but the lovers in the room refused to notice him and his angry knock, rather he only heard more clearly Annie's scream and the pounding of Winthrop's penis in Annie's young pleasure spot. When Gerrard noticed he was getting hard which wasn't good for him since there wasn't relief in sight, he quickly ran back to the room and stuffed his ears to avoid hearing tempestuous sounds from crazy lovers. From the position on the floor, Winthrop took Annie to the oak table in his room, Annie's eyes shone brightly with intense enjoyment and Unbridled excitement, Winthrop was giving it to her with a touch of perfection, just the way she wanted it. She loved not just sex but good sex and Winthrop's sex was not just good, it was great. On getting Annie to the table, he removed every tiny thing on the table, Annie helped him fling his armor which was obstructing the space away when he was sure the table was completely bare, he lay Annie flat on it and used his fingers to spread the outer lips of her vagina, he fingered her clitoris vigorously, making her squirm and Squirt, as Annie's hips bounced on the table in intense pleasure, he walked away from her, went to the ice bucket in his room, took a bottle of malt whiskey and drank several drops of it, he was trying to obtain more energy and intoxicate his brain, he gave Annie some for herself and she willingly drank it for she understood perfectly the effect it would have on her. The whiskey was meant to make her hornier and postpone her climax. After Annie had taken a good quantity of the drink, Winthrop poured some of the whiskey on her body, then he proceeded to suck it off her, from her nipples, eyes, throat, navel, etc, then he went back to her honey pot and spread it for his grand entrance, he stroked his hard rod and drove it into her wetness nearly hitting Annie's womb, his target was to hit and give Annie's womb soft strokes, so he withdrew his hard erection and rammed it in again, this time with full force and hit his target, Annie screamed, lifted her upper body off the bed and hugged him tightly, begging him to screw her hard and mercilessly. Winthrop loved hard screwing so he obeyed Annie and started dancing energetically in between her shaking legs. For several minutes, he concentrated on softly hitting her womb and creating electricity in her honey pot. The sweat that covered them trickled into their mouths and eyes, stinging their eyes with its saltiness yet they persisted, for the pleasure they created was sweeter than honey and made every discomfort quite insignificant. Then Winthrop went faster and faster, he was panting like a bull and moving his hips inside Annie's pleasure pot like a manipulated machine, then he exploded inside her, filling her, yet he continued moving his hips but this time slowly until Annie hit cloud nine and shook helplessly, for the pleasure traveled around her veins and settled at her brain. When the intense cloud nine pleasure receded, they lay on Winthrop's bed with Annie's head on his chest, they had no intention of quitting their erotic escapade, Nah, their rest was to accumulate more energy and go for a second round. Winthrop stroked Annie's hair lovingly, he loved the naughty Annie, the only girl who could stand and match his sexual stamina, other ladies always cried after more than one hour, some of them would cover their pleasure spot protectively with their palms after he had screwed them raw some would even wear their robes and run away, one particular damsel after taking close to two hours of hot Unbridled sex ran out of Winthrop's room without bothering to wear her robe, the fire in between her legs made her reckless so she pushed Winthrop aside, stood up from the bed and ran off into the night, for he had taken her under raw and tirelessly as though they were going to die that night. How she got home Winthrop did not know, but he wasn't very happy with the girl for his hardness stood erect without release for several minutes until he was forced to wear his robe and stroll around the vast castle with his hardness erect as a statue, that night he could hardly find sleep for as he lay on his bed, his hardness pointed aggressively to the roof. Sweet Annie never left him hanging, she always had more than enough stamina to take his rock-hard thrust, she didn't just take it, she always raised her hips to welcome the thrust and would roll her hips as he grinds her. He stroked Annie's hair further, rubbing his palm gently on her firm beautiful body. Then like a flash Annie rose from the bed and took over. With Winthrop lying flat on the bed, she straddled him with the agility of a monkey and stroked him gently but expertly until his masculine length became hard and aggressive, then she rose slightly and placed her moist ever-horny vagina on its tips, teasing him until Winthrop begged her to sit on his hardness, she teased him a little more by rubbing his hardness around the entrance of her pleasure spot without allowing him to thrust it in, when Winthrop started begging her pitifully to please sit on his sleek hardness, she took pity on him and descended on his big shiny hardness, the warmth, and moistness of her honey pot was so sweet that Winthrop closed his eyes, sighing with pleasure. For a few seconds, she sat on his hardness without moving, Winthrop opened his eyes and pleaded again for her to start moving already, she only smiled mischievously and refused to move, he promised her all the gold the Duke would pay him at the end of the month yet she refused to move, he threatened to screw her for more than four hours yet she refused to move, she only smiled tAuntingly at him, daring him to screw her to hell. Then as Winthrop was almost close to tears in frustration, she started moving her hips most seductively and expertly, Winthrop's hardness danced inside her vagina while she bounced on him like a puppet being pulled by an entertainer, her hair flew in all angles as she bounced and covered her face, she could see glistening sweat on Winthrop's body and hers yet she wasn't deterred. On and on she bounced, taking his hardness completely inside her and compressing it with the tightness of her vagina walls. Winthrop's eyes closed again as the pleasure saturated his body, he could only feel the Sweetness they created as she bounced tirelessly on his body and did her sexual magic. Then she started bouncing faster and a few seconds later Winthrop started groaning, they knew they were going to hit cloud nine together and it pleased them greatly, just when they didn't expect it, both of them climaxed and held each other tightly as Annie collapsed on his body tired and completely drenched with sweat. They were so tired that they both promptly fell asleep with satisfied smiles on their faces. Meanwhile, the nameless witch was at the upper part of the castle demanding where Gastard kept the green bottle while Gastard searched his bed-chamber from one corner to the other. As Gastard sweated at the angry question of the witch, Claire was still with her newfound friend at the royal garden. It was different strokes for different folks that night. Gastard's world was collapsing, Winthrop and Annie had the best sex of their lives while Claire found for herself, a strange but interesting friend. The knights kept watch and were battle-ready, they waited for the beast to emerge from the garden but it didn't for over an hour, at a point they assumed the beast had fallen asleep and one of them suggested that they tiptoe to the garden to see for themselves but before they could take a step, they heard a low howl from the beast and knew that it was very much awake but was intent on remaining at the garden. As Gastard searched for the bottle, he wondered why the she-wolf didn't howl under his window, as usual, he assumed that it was because the witch was in the room with him. In the garden, Claire was trying to talk to the beast. She smiled and asked.

"Can you speak?"

The beast only stared at her blankly, so she made signs at the beast and yet it did not understand but when she said.

"Are you my best friend, you do have her eyes?" the beast stood strangely still and looked at her with narrowed eyes as if it understood the word friend.

Claire's heart beat wildly with anticipation but the beast didn't give any answer, Claire felt disappointed but asked again in a low voice "Were you ever human?"

The she-wolf relaxed her face into what looked like a smile but said nothing, so Claire knew it couldn't speak and maybe didn't even understand her words but she found her new friend very interesting, all fears she had earlier about the beast had vanished, all she knew was that the comfort she felt around the beast was the type one feels around friends, she heard herself promising the beast to be its friend. The beast swished its tail like it understood, at a point, Claire felt foolish for talking to a beast and giggled to herself. Ever since Gastard took her captive and barred her family and friends from visiting her, she hadn't had a conversation except for the few times Gastard or anyone in the castle directed a question at her. In the evenings, when Gastard was done with all state affairs and was free for discussions, she avoided him and his aggressive penis, so talking to the she-wolf was a much-needed pleasure especially as the beast was listening intently, which was encouraging so she talked on and on. She told the beast of how she missed her parents and how she missed producing fragrant perfumes with her mother and selling those perfumes to her favorite customers at the Zazu market, how she missed strolling around Zazu in the evenings with her fellow maidens, she intensely missed swimming in the deep Zazu lake, as she talked, the beast listened patiently. She also talked of those first few weeks after Gastard took her captive when she requested to be allowed to go to the Zazu lake to swim but Gastard told her she was the queen and wasn't supposed to swim in an open lake like a commoner, rather he ordered the maids to put sweet smelling fragrances in the royal pool and told her to go and swim there as much as she liked. The royal pool was beautiful, its walls were tiled with gold and it smelt like one of those fragrances that her mother produced, she appreciated it but frankly wanted to swim in a natural pool, a fast-flowing river, where she could compete with the fishes while swimming. As a child, she and her friends had competed with the fishes while swimming, they swam fast, trying their best to out-swim the small fishes in the lake but Gastard would not let her swim in the lake for he feared that she may intentionally drown herself since he wouldn't let her go home or she may escape the vigilance of his guards and run away, so in the castle, Claire stayed without crossing its walls. The castle was majestic and she had everything she wanted and more except her freedom, the free-dom every human deserves. All these she told the beast and it lis-tened or better still appeared to listen to her. The she-wolf stared at her intently as if it understood her words. Then Claire men-tioned how Gastard always invaded her pussy without her per-mission with his big lengthy hardness. Immediately those words were out of her mouth, the beast started howling very loudly, its eyes started taking that red hot hue that scared every human, Claire became frightened and attempted to rise from the hairy legs of the beast where she lay but the beast stared down at her with those red hot eyes, those glittering eyes that were as hot as hell and Claire stayed still, quivering in every limb. The knights on hearing the howl of the beast held their swords firmly, ready for battle. Claire could feel the incredible rage and energy eman-ating from the beast's body yet it did not attack her, rather the beast nudged Claire and she stood up from its legs, then like a flash the beast was gone, it ran close to the castle walls, scaled it and disappeared into the night. The knights saw it go and heaved sighs of relief, their eyes were heavy with sleep, and the vigilance they kept weighed heavily on their bodies, those brave warriors re-tired to their quarters to get a well-deserved rest, they knew the beast wouldn't return that night, it appeared and prowled only once every night, so they were certain it wasn't coming back. After the knights retired for the knight, Claire folded her blanket hurriedly and crept back into the castle, she was nearly busted by Gastard who was descending the stairs, followed by the witch who was complaining of something Claire didn't wish to hear. She entered her room breathing hard and dived under the duvet waiting for sleep to get her but the strange friend she found that night and the thought of what could happen when the bottle was discovered to be missing kept her awake. She was sure that the witch and Gastard were looking for the bottle and maybe were already at each other's neck about it. Then fear entered her body as she thought of the consequences of her action. Should she be caught, the witch may even in a fit of rage turn her into something more hideous than a wolf, maybe her soul will be trapped forever inside the body of a hyena, goose pimples filled her skin as she thought of these terrible things. When she could think no more, she closed her eyes and gradually drifted off to sleep. When the witch and Gastard came down, the witch told him that she could stay no more and was leaving since Gastard couldn't take care of a little green bottle, Gastard went down on his knees and asked for her help. It didn't bother him that he was the Duke and wasn't supposed to be kneeling for his subject, but then the subject before whom he knelt had the power to destroy his life and raze his vast kingdom to the ground. He didn't know what punishment the spirits the witch served would inflict on him for misplacing the green bottle, so he went on his knees and begged the witch for help but there was nothing the witch could and she told him so. There was only one option she told him, the option of burying the green bottle, to permanently tie a human soul with that of a wolf. The failure of this magic exercise was bound to destroy Gastard. That was the verdict of the spirits and there was nothing even the witch could do about it. When Gastard wouldn't stop pleading, the witch decided to stay at the castle for more than twenty-four hours to give the Duke ample time to find the bottle. Gastard stood up with gratitude, he was confident he would find the bottle and bury it at the stroke of midnight the next day. He took the witch to one of the numerous guest rooms in his castle and retired to his private chamber with a heavy heart. He could feel his enviable life coming to an end, but worried that if he died, the virgins of the world may remain unfucked, which troubled and saddened him as he lay down to sleep. He decided he was going to search his whole castle until he found the elusive green bottle.

CHAPTER TWELVE

The next day, the whole castle was in a frenzy, the Duke was frantically searching all the rooms in his castle while the witch followed him around, muttering curses all along. Gastard's guards were with him too they turned all rooms upside down, leaving no stone unturned. When they searched the rooms at the upper level of the castle and found nothing, Gastard's eyes became bloodshot with rage, he could hear the witch growing impatient and threatening to leave at the expiration of twenty - four hours. When Gastard and his guards were sure that the green bottle wasn't in any of the rooms upstairs, they marched downstairs, the witch was too indignant to continue with what she suspected was going to be a fruitless search, so she sat down in the duke's opulent sitting room with crossed her legs, refusing to be bothered any further by what she termed the duke's personal problems. Aunt Marvy who was relaxing in the sitting room stood up almost immediately and left the sitting room, the witch sneered at her as she left but made no move to stop her for the witch needed the whole sitting room to herself. She wanted to think about the whole disappearance of the green bottle she gave the Duke, perhaps if she had known that Claire and the Duke slept in the same room, she would have smelt a rat but she didn't know that piece of indie, she thought Claire had her room and only visited the Duke for pleasure purposes. She knew no one would dare enter the duke's private chamber without permission and Winthrop always stood on guard outside the duke's private chambers, even in the duke's absence. So what happened to that bottle? The witch asked herself frowning deeply. When she could find no answer, she concluded that it was the duke's stupidity that led to the disappearance of the bottle, she considered him careless indeed because he understood the importance of the bottle and still let it slip away from his grasp. When a servant passed, she ordered the servant to get her breakfast for before that moment, she was too busy with the search to eat, even Gastard was yet to break his fast which was understandable, only Claire and Aunt Marvy dined at the Castle's dining hall, the both of them ate their breakfast thinking the Duke and the witch would join them later. Claire knew what the hullabaloo was all about and it pleased her that she had rocked the duke's pitch-perfect world. Aunt Marvy sitting across her was in the dark and repeatedly asked Claire what the matter with the Duke was, Claire only said that the Duke was perhaps looking for something important when Aunt Marvy queried her on what the important thing was, Claire said she had no idea. So sitting in the grand sitting room in the royal castle, the witch had her breakfast, the Duke and his problems could go to hell as far as she was concerned. Meanwhile, the search continued downstairs, they found Claire lying on her bed downstairs and politely asked her to leave the room for a moment, obediently she left and the guards took over, they lifted all heavy furniture and searched like their lives depended on it, when they got to the wardrobe, their search became pleasurable for Claire had some sweet looking panties lying in the wardrobe, the guards winked at each other on seeing that, their search had yielded something beautiful and they wanted more of it, only Gastard paced the room worriedly, he was too worried to notice the panties and the pleasure it gave his guards. From Claire's room they moved to Aunt Marvy's, she too was asked to kindly leave her room, at first she wanted to complain about it, she knew nothing was hidden in her room but the cold rage in the duke's eyes stopped her and reluctantly she stepped out, again the guards searched thoroughly as before and again they found more undies and panties to pleasure their sight. They took time to shake off the undies to Gastard. They were doing a good job shaking out every clothing that could contain or hide the object of their search but to the guards, shaking out those undies was a much-needed relief in the strenuous search they were burdened with. The Duke was growing weary but he persisted in the search, the witch had given her final word that she would leave at the expiration of twenty - four hours and Gastard knew there was no talking her out of it, so he followed the guards as they searched all the rooms and proceeded to the servants quarters. Most of the servants were females, so the guards looked forward to searching their rooms. They barged into the first room and saw two maids intently poking each other's vagina and giggling excitedly, they were entwined on the bed, dipping their fingers into their young pussies and enjoying themselves, when the guards barged in, they sprang apart with fright, the Duke entered next. and they ran off through the back door without bothering to wear their robes even though it was daytime, such as the intensity of their fright. The Duke though worried and enraged about his missing bottle found himself smiling at the girls, the guards did better than smile, they howled with laughter patting each other at the back, their search was becoming wonderful indeed. They searched the room and again found nothing. On and on the search continued, they searched all the servants quarters yet nothing was found, one unfortunate maid was found taking her bath when the guards barged in, the naughty guards entered her bathroom with the excuse that they urgently needed to see if what the Duke wanted was in her bathroom, the Duke himself didn't stop them, despite his situation, he couldn't resist seeing a naked girl, so he let his guards barge into the maid's bathroom. The young maid tried to cover her freshly shaven pussy with her small palms, one guard squeezed her nipples when the duke's face was turned away, the maid splashed water on him and the other guards laughed. The search party moved on to the quarters reserved for the knights of the Zazu empire. It bothered Gastard that he had to search the quarters of the knights for he knew that they were men of honor who swore an oath to serve Zazu till their death, brave warriors who could never steal from the Duke but the green bottle needed to be found and urgently too, so the Duke accompanied by his guards who looked afraid of entering the knights quarters marched in and after the Duke had briefly addressed the knights, the search started, some of the knights in their usual spirit of servitude to the empire joined in the search and just as expected, the search yielded nothing. If the bottle was ever found, it would never be in the knight's quarters.

A weary and dejected Gastard called a meeting of everyone living in his castle, when everyone was gathered, the Duke promised anyone who would find the bottle a hundred bars of gold and several plots of land. The reward was mouth-watering and Gastard knew it. He wanted all the castle dwellers to keep an eye out for his precious bottle, also he ordered his guards to send a message to his scribes that the Duke wanted their audience immediately, the scribes of the empire answered the summon of their Duke with an immediate speed that was admirable, when they assembled, they waited for the duke's decree with their hands poised to write every word from the Duke on their writing pad. Gastard looked around and made sure that the twenty-four scribes that represent the twenty-four provinces of Zazu were present, then he gave his decree that he the imperil Duke of Zazu was offering a reward of a hundred bars of gold, coupled with several plots of land to anyone who would find a bottle that was green in color and corked with a magical substance, he told his scribes that the bottle and its content was for an important ritual that would protect Zazu from her enemies and ensure the continued progress of the empire. Gastard knew that the people of Zazu were inseparably attached to the wealth of the empire, so was sure that telling them that the bottle was going to be used in a ritual that would prosper Zazu was all the encouragement his people needed to search the nooks and crannies of Zazu for the bottle. The twenty-four scribes penned down his instructions and swiftly headed back to their respective provinces to disperse the message. When they left, Gastard gave in to his weariness and demanded food, the chefs quickly served him, fearing that he might transfer his aggression to them should they delay for a second but before Gastard had his breakfast, he sent another guard to invite immediately all the Lords of the empire to his castle. While he broke his fast, he felt a strong need for a woman, he needed relief from the anger and disappointment bottled inside him, those emotions were too strong to stay in his heart so he decided to relieve himself Pleasantly and when he thought of pleasure, his thoughts went to the beautiful Claire, the love of his life, Claire with the bouncy arse. He hurried his breakfast and went in search of Claire, he found her in her room downstairs and led her gently upstairs to his private chamber. Claire was shocked that the Duke thought of sex when his life was literally in a mess, she wanted to complain that she wasn't in the mood for sexual frolics and the aggressiveness of his penis but the intensity of the need in the duke's eyes shut her up and so like a meek sweet lover, she followed him to his chamber knowing pretty well what was waiting for her once he closed his mighty door. The moment they were behind the door, the Duke swiftly unrobed himself and threw those constraining robes far away from his person, then he reached for Claire with savage hunger, cradling her soft body to his chest, he removed her robe and in his haste tore her undies to shreds, Claire gasped with surprise at the urgency of his need. When Gastard saw Claire's pink clitoris sticking out of her fresh young pussy, he went wild and lifted her off her legs, he kept her gently on his grand dressing table, went down on one knee, and sucked at Claire's protruding tender clitoris, Claire held his head as the Sweetness shot through her like an arrow, from the center of her honey pot to the center of her brain. As Gastard sucked harder, giving her clitoris tiny tender lovers bite, she held his head stronger so she wouldn't fall for the

Sweetness of his touch was shaking her legs vigorously, as vigorously as a mighty wind shakes the bouncy arse of an endowed woman, Gastard tortured her clitoris until it became slippery and raw, then he delved his tongue Indus the walls of her sweet pussy, he rolled his tongue inside her as if he was licking candy, Claire screamed wildly before she could stop herself, for her honey pot was under pleasurable siege, Gastard quickly removed his face as Claire squirted all over his dressing table, then he carried her to his vast bed and feasted on her nipples while fondling the roundness of her full breast, he ate those nipples like they were tangerine while Claire moaned louder and louder when the nipples turned crimson due to the intensity of his touch, he placed tiny kisses from her breast to her navel while Claire squirmed with pleasure on the bed. She hated the man doing the erotic magic on her body yet, he always set her body on fire whenever he touched her. He was indeed the unchallenged god of sex, when Gastard got to her honey pot, he covered the lips of her vagina with one hard kiss before stroking his erection which was already as hard as a brick, and pointing aggressively forward. Then he put a soft pillow under Claire's arse and entered her with one mighty thrust, the room turned briefly across Claire's eyes, then she focused on Gastard's lusty eyes as he screwed her honey pot, grinding it hard and sending her back and forth to paradise, just when Claire thought he was going to give her a brief pause, he pounded her harder, hitting her soft pussy with his iron hard hardness, she placed her lower palms across her lower navel for he was hitting her womb repeatedly with his sexual acrobatics, Gastard withdrew his penis and as Claire exhaled thinking it was all over, he entered her again, pounding her harder and stronger, meanwhile the Lords of Zazu were already gathered and were waiting at the palace in answer to the urgent summons of their Duke, when they told a guard to inform the Duke that they were waiting, the guard politely said that the Duke could not be disturbed at the moment, the Lords who knew the ever horny hormones of the Duke understood that he was on top of a maiden. Some of them relaxed thinking there was no problem since the

Duke had the penis to seek pleasure after summoning his Lords so urgently and equally found time to enjoy a woman's warmth but lord Henry knew better, he knew the Duke could be pursued by all the demons of hell and still find time to screw a pretty damsel, the duke's adventure with his wife, while he was in prison, was all the proof he needed to agree that Gastard was a fuckaholic without boundaries, a Duke who was always on heat and so while the other Lords relaxed waiting for the Duke, Lord Henry thought of who the Duke was possibly screwing at the moment, he wondered if it was his wife who he sent packing and who was, therefore, free to continue with her sexual exploits with the Duke. Maybe another innocent virgin was taking the pounding of his erection, stretched out immovably under him, lord Henry sighed in anger and wished he could cut off the ever-horny erection of the Duke meanwhile the Duke in his private chambers spread Claire's legs wider and pounded the soft folds of her honey pot energetically, he lifted her beautiful legs high into the air and inserted his hardness into the moist pink vagina lips of Claire, at that moment, Claire squirted again, covering the rich embroidered Egyptian bedsheet with her natural Juice but Gastard wouldn't spare her yet, just as she finished squirting, he rammed his rod into her and screwed her pussy with her legs lifted high up while Claire's moans filled the whole bed chamber and drifted over to the ears of whoever cared to listen. Gastard loved his Claire and couldn't get enough of her, he opened her legs as it was still lifted high in the air and pounded her faster and faster, by then Claire had climaxed severally but Gastard was yet to find his orgasm, he rode her like a sexualized driver and when his body couldn't take the Sweetness anymore, he climaxed, filling her up completely with his Juice. He collapsed on Claire, holding her tight and lovingly. Claire herself was completely spent, so she allowed him to cuddle her protectively while dropping tiny kisses on her hair, still, the Lords at the palace waited, one of them said fuckaholic under his breath and the Lords burst out laughing, they understood that the comment referred to their Duke and they agreed that he was a chronic, incorrigible, fuckaholic. When the Duke rested a while with Claire in his arms, he ordered Winthrop who unfailingly was standing guard outside his door to get him a bottle of wine and small chops. He knew he had drained Claire's energy for his energy was spent too. When the drink and chops arrived, he fed Claire lovingly for she was too tired to feed herself. The Duke loved Claire daily and was very glad to feed her. He wished she would agree to be his forever so that he would dance in between her legs forever, most of all, he wished that the green bottle will be found, so that the innocent soul trapped in the wolf's body will be damned forever without hope of redemption. When they finished eating, the Duke went leisurely to the bathroom for a quick shower, and still, the Lords waited to curse his raging hormones and randiness under their breath.

CHAPTER THIRTEEN

5. She missed her love for years

Missed the warmth of her breast and curly hairs

The softness of her bosom and tender cares

The wetness of her paradise and seductive stares

10. The fulness of her bosom

And the roundness of her bottom.

While the Lords waited for the Duke to condescend to join them, they tried to stifle their hunger because they knew they wouldn't be fed by the royal chefs until the Duke had dismissed them and so they complained under their breaths but waited for their Duke, when Gastard eventually joined them after they had lost all hope of ever seeing him, he walked haughtily yo his throne without any apology whatsoever, hr looked refreshed and contented and looked at his Lords like they were children waiting at his pleasure, the contentment on his face told his Lords that he just had a good fuck and some of them were jealous, the Duke looked grand indeed and had just had a good screw while they were condemned to wait interminably for him. Gastard knew that if his Lords were not happy then lord Henry was the unhappiest of them all, for he knew lord Henry hadn't forgiven him after his bedroom escapade with his wife. Zazu Lords weren't surprised at the lack of courtesy of their young Duke, they were used to it, they would have been stunned if he had apologized for keeping them waiting after hastily dragging them out of their respective houses. On behalf of the Lords, Lord Winston, the eldest of all the Lords and was therefore according to the sacred customs of Zazu the prime minister of Zazu empire politely asked Gastard why he had summoned them, Gastard told them of his missing green bottle and how he desperately needed it for an important ritual that was going to be productive to the whole of Zazu, while he spoke the witch entered and the meeting broke apart, the Lords didn't know that the nameless witch was within the environs of the royal castle, therefore her sudden entrance into the palace was as shocking as a lion let loose in a busy street, some of the Lords attempted to leave much to the delight of the witch, it pleased her that men trembled at her footsteps and scurried away from her like rats, Gastard assured the panic-stricken Lords that they were safe and that the witch was there to help them. Fearfully they returned to their seats, not fully sure of the truthfulness of the duke's words, the witch walked gracefully to a seat and made herself comfortable, the atmosphere was instantly tense, most of the Lords became self-conscious they didn't want her trouble and wished she would just go away, Gastard continued with his speech and asked the Lords if they had any solution for him. Maybe if the witch wasn't in their midst, they would have thought of a good antidote to the duke's problem but the witch was very much present and their brains refused to work, they concentrated on not annoying her so as not to fall victim to her rage which was famed to be hotter than hell. To make matters worse, the witch gathered her flowing robe, she lifted it above her knees and crossed her legs, she was just trying to relax but unknown to her, her robe opened dangerously below her legs and the lord seated across from her could see the tantalizing triangle in between her legs, the witch hardly wore undies, so the lord seated opposite her saw the shape and color of her honey pot, the lord was very uncomfortable, for he knew the witch would turn him into something hideous if she caught him staring but he couldn't stop staring and the witch wouldn't close her legs. The Duke told his Lords to encourage the people in their respective provinces to please search the nooks and crannies of the empire and find his missing very important bottle. Lord Winston on behalf of the Lords assured the Duke that they were going to play their parts and help to find the duke's bottle. In unison, the Lords rose and headed to the banquet hall for their entertainment for that was the norm after each meeting with the Duke, the custom said they were to be richly fed each time they burdened their heads with the empire's troubles, it was one of the perks of being a lord in a rich empire like Zazu. After the Lords rose and left, the witch rose too not knowing that a certain lord had already spied her clitoris shining bright at the center of her enticing pussy, and luckily for him, he wasn't caught. The witch left the palace and went into the sitting room, she had attended the meeting thinking the Lords were going to make a useful contribution to the present crisis but she realized too late that her presence caged their tongues and sealed their mouths. When everyone left the palace, the Duke was left alone to think about his misfortune, meanwhile, time was running out.

By evening after the duke met with his Lords, two maidens came with two bottles covered with sand and demanded to see the Duke, the maidens looked excited, they were sure they had found the bottle the Duke wanted, they were pretty sure that one of the bottles was the one their Duke wanted for the bottles were discolored and looked quite queer. The Duke who was in a heated discussion with the witch was informed that two maidens brought bottles that looked like what he wanted. The Duke rushed out with a racing heart, hoping to find his misplaced treasure, the two maidens presented their bottles with wide smiles, the Duke ordered that the bottles be washed so that their actual colors would be seen when the bottles were cleaned up and returned, the Duke was sorely disappointed, they weren't the ones he wanted, he managed to control his rage and waved the maidens away after instructing a guard to give them a bar of gold each for their troubles, the guards were also instructed to bring to the duke's attention, anything the people brought to the Duke, Gastard was determined to find his bottle and didn't mind checking out anything that was brought to him. The guard that showed the maidens the way out of the castle took the liberty to press them against the castle wall and squeezed their breasts for bringing false information, the maidens still clutching their gold scratched the guard's back as he pressed their young breasts, they ran away from the indecent guard who stood by the castle gate waiting for more maidens to enter his trap. When Claire heard that some maidens brought some bottles that matched the one the Duke wanted, she was scared that her bottle had been seen and found, so while the Duke spoke with the maidens downstairs, she peeked at them from the window upstairs, critically examining their bottles to see if one of them was the bottle she hid among the thick flower hedges in the garden. Thankfully, none of the bottles was the right one, she exhaled in relief and went back to her room but she made sure she listened to the conversations around her. When the Duke informed the witch that none of the bottles was the right one, she bluntly reminded him that she was leaving the next morning, so he had better find his bottle. The guards in the castle were busy all evening, they kept inspecting all bottles the people brought and took the bottles to the Duke for identification, by the time they checked the two hundredth bottle, they were weary while the Duke gave up hope of ever finding his green bottle. The witch on her part was just waiting for a new day to dawn so that she would go back to the caves she loved. She was sure her numerous gods and his goddesses had missed her and were beginning to wonder where their priestess was, during dinner that evening, the Duke had no appetite but the witch, Claire, and Aunt Marvy attacked their meals with gusto, it wasn't their fault that things were the way they were, besides the dinner was top-notch, as usual, the royal chefs were the best in kitchen affairs, so the three women attacked their smoked salmon and fresh fruits salad, taking care to top their meal with the bottles of excellent claret chilling in buckets of ice, they ignored the solemn Duke completely, he was the Duke so if he didn't want to eat that was completely his business besides Aunt Marvy needed strength for the self-imposed task ahead of her, she was expecting her baby May later that evening and she needed the energy to suck her baby's honey pot, young firm breast, and navel. She intended to finger May until she saw stars and rub their vaginas together until both vaginas were locked and grinding together, she needed strength for all these so she ate heartily and allowed the chefs to refill her wine glass, meanwhile the golden goblet that Gastard drank with remained empty, he sat at the head of the table, barely tasting his meal, just brooding and refusing to be made happy. As the evening became darker and stars shone, the diners finished and Claire went to her room for a scented bath, she was going to visit her she-wolf friend at the midnight hour, so she decided to freshen up and sleep awhile. Aunt Marvy too retired hastily, she excitedly anticipated May's arrival, the witch too had an agenda, she had her eyes on Winthrop for she observed him closely and felt he had a big dick beneath the well-cut leather uniform all guards wore, she observed all day and decided she was going to see if her suspicions were right. So when she finished her dinner, she retired to the guest room where she slept the previous night and showered too, she took her time scrubbing her skin with scented soap so that Winthrop would see only the beauty of her skin and not the magic she was capable of. When the evening grew dark enough, boldly the witch went in search of Winthrop while May sneaked into Aunt Marvy's room, the Duke was sitting deject- edly in the sitting room downstairs saw their movements and felt very sorry for himself, everyone was going to have fun except him, he felt his pleasure tool and discovered that his ever aggres- sive penis was for the first time lying limp underneath his robe. Someone was going to get an erection that night and it wasn't him, he was sure the witch was going to find for herself a lover for the night before retiring to her lonely caves, the thought sad- dened Gastard greatly, he wished the bottle would just be found so that his world would return to its erotic normalcy. The Duke and his problems notwithstanding, Aunt Marvy grabbed the beautiful May as she entered her room and lifted the young maid off her feet, May giggled and planted a sweet kiss on Aunt Marvy's lips. Aunt Marvy brought her down and put her hands beneath May's nightdress, she was very glad to see that May wore nothing underneath, taking swift advantage of the situation, Aunt Marvy dipped two fingers into May's wet pussy and fingered her clitoris, May squirmed with pleasure and would have fallen if Aunt May hadn't grabbed her, holding her gently to herself. She led May to the big bed and removed the girl's nightdress, revealing May's young beautiful body. Aunt Marvy undressed in a flash and descended hungrily on May, she dipped two fingers again into May's wet vagina, rubbing her clitoris vigorously while May at the same time sucked Aunt Marvy's big watermelon breast. They simultaneously gave and received pleasure from each other, with their eyes shining excitedly, Aunt Marvy increased the number of fingers in May's honey pot to four and May went crazy, she sucked harder on Aunt Marvy's breast while using her left hand to cup the other big breast. When Aunt Marvy's fingers were dripping with, she straddled May tightly until her honey pot was against May's honey pot than she gradually began to move, rubbing their clitoris together while sparks blew in their brains, May held Aunt Marvy's arse tighter, urging her to move faster and stronger, that was the kind of instruction Aunt Marvy liked, so she obeyed May and moved faster until their vaginas were making obscene noises. Then May flipped Aunt Marvy over and attacked the fleshy mound of Aunt Marvy's vagina with her tongue. The witch walked out of the main castle building which housed the Duke and his family and walked towards the quarters meant for the guards, the castle guards that saw her coming scampered away, unknown to them, the witch was horny and not in the mood to kill or maim, boldly she walked into the guards quarters and asked for Winthrop. The guard who answered the witch was stricken with fear but had enough wits to say he didn't know where Winthrop was, then the witch remembered that Winthrop had the task of standing guard outside the private chambers of the Duke, very quickly, she turned around and headed back to the castle's main building like a bitch on heat. She went upstairs look-ing for Winthrop, Gastard saw her agitatedly looking for someone and became sadder, it wasn't him she or any lady was looking for, why should he be happy? Winthrop who was dedicatedly guard-ing the duke's private chambers saw the witch approaching and froze in fear, he didn't know why she was coming towards him with the bold stare on her face, he thought that he was going to die, very boldly the witch walked up to Winthrop and pinned him to the wall. She saw the profound fear in his eyes so she smiled and saw him relax.

"I'm horny, could you help please?" she whispered into his ears.

Winthrop's eyes grew round with ecstasy, he could hardly believe his luck, among Zazu men, the witch was seen to be untouchable and frankly above their reach but right there before his very eyes, the witch's full bosom was pressed to his chest, the warm mound of her pussy was pressed against the section of his robe where his manhood lay when the witch saw that Winthrop continued smil-ing at her with a shocked grin on his face, she asked him again,

"Would you like to fuck?" that question hit home and spurred Winthrop into action.

"Yes, I mean Oh! Yes, I would very much like to fuck" Winthrop hastily answered so that the witch wouldn't change her mind.

She led him downstairs to her room, they needed to pass the grand sitting room before getting to the witch's sitting room and so when they got to the sitting room, the witch held Winthrop's hand tighter for she knew he would panic on seeing the Duke, just as she predicted, Winthrop saw the Duke sitting alone sadly in the sitting room and his lost senses came back, he remembered he wasn't supposed to leave his duty post unless the Duke expressly permitted him, he tried to extricate his hand from the witch's grasp but the witch assured him that the Duke wouldn't mind, he looked fearfully at the Duke and their eyes locked,

"I was just trying to explain to the priestess sir that I'm not allowed to leave my duty post," Winthrop said to the Duke but the Duke simply waved his hand in dismissal.

He didn't care about what anyone did, he only wanted to find his missing bottle or be left alone. With the Duke completely uninterested in whatever they planned to do, Winthrop eagerly followed the witch to her room, the door was barely closed behind them when the witch squatted on her knee and removed the lower part of winthrop's robe, his lengthy fat manhood dangled out like a ringing bell and the witch smiled, she liked what she saw and knew she was going to enjoy herself tremendously, her pussy was going to be filled to the brim, she took winthrop's long, fat manhood gently in her palms and put it inside her mouth, her mouth was very warm and soft and as she closed her lips around winthrop's length, his whole body squirmed with pleasure, it was like his body floated in space, she held the witch's head and at the same instant, her head started moving back and forth on his manhood, she licked, sucked and ran her tongue lovingly on his lengthy rod until he grew hard, she increased the tempo of her tongue movement on his warm rod until he grew from hard to aggressive, then she released his length and stood up but Winthrop grabbed her begging for more, she laughed and disentangled herself from him, seductively she removed her robe and her round arse shook freely, winthrop's eyes nearly bulged out of his head as he beheld the perfect roundness of her body, he removed the upper part of his robe and waited eagerly for her to give the signal that she was ready to be screwed till she saw the stars.

CHAPTER FOURTEEN

5. Everyone deserves a good screw.

Heated electricity from nature's brew.

If you want some follow my cue.

Let's create some erotic hues!

10. If happiness is life

Then life is sex, for sex is happiness without strife.

The witch climbed her bed, knelt on the center and positioned her round arse for Winthrop, from the door Winthrop jumped into the bed for he was in a hurry, he knelt behind the witch, bent her forward until her pussy was sticking up to him, then he urgently guided his hardened erection into her moist pussy, the warmth there was a perfect welcome for his horny hardness, he took a deep breath and began thrusting into the quivering vagina of the witch, as he thrust in, the witch made cat-like noises, he thrust in deeper and the witch's pussy greedily sucked him in, on and on they continued and then he increased the tempo from thrusting to pounding, he pounded her like an ironsmith pounded metals, the witch bared her teeth in enjoyment, she spread her knees wider and started rolling her hips to match his pounding, she was good with her hips and Winthrop knew how to stroke a woman's pussy, ge turned her over and before she could breathe, he entered her again, thrashing wildly inside the folds of her honey pot and at the same time his tongue found her nipples of those big and rounded breasts, as he powerfully pounded her pussy, his tongue performed sorcery on her nipples and this time the witch was the victim, he licked and bit her nipples, for the witch was a dream come true, from her nipples he moved up to her sensual lips and kissed her passionately, then he kissed her eyes and stuck his tongue into her ear, that was the witch's favorite spot, a lover's tongue in her ear always drove her crazy, she held him tightly, moaning like she had no care in the world. While he kissed her eyes, throat, ears, and mouth, his hips never stopped thrusting into her wet vagina, for several minutes they rocked each other's world, and an hour later they were still at it. Meanwhile, Aunt Marvy and May had sucked each other senseless, they took turns sucking each other's vagina and biting each other's clitoris until that piece of pink flesh was raw and pink, they had their orgasm in each other's arms and at that moment, Aunt Marvy knew she couldn't live without May, she decided she was going to ask May to spend the rest of her life with her, that was her moment and she boldly took it.

"Would you like to spend your life with me like forever?" Aunt Marvy fearfully asked because she feared May would turn her down. May scanned Aunt Marvy's face for a while, wondering if she was been pranked but Aunt Marvy's eyes held nothing but love and so it dawned on May that Aunt Marvy was very serious, her eyes filled with tears, she never thought that one day she would find love among her gender, she had previously thought that happiness was beyond her, now not only had she found love but it was coming from royalty too, a thing she never thought was possible in her lifetime.

"Yes, I love you too and I'll like to grow old with you," May said in a teary voice and Aunt Marvy hugged her tight for a very long time.

She had found a soul mate after death took her first love away leaving her desolate. She stroked May's hair tenderly and planted soft kisses on her forehead. Meanwhile, Winthrop thrust hard and long into the witch's pussy, he would withdraw his hardness and thrust it in again hard and strong, this he continued to do until the witch screamed as she hit cloud nine and floated out of her body but Winthrop wouldn't spare her, he continued to hit her hard until he was overtaken with enjoyment and spilled his seed right into the soft folds of her pussy. The witch so enjoyed Winthrop's love-making that she drew him into a sweet hug, Winthrop cuddled her gently in his arms and locked that way they drifted off to sleep. Shortly before the midnight hour, Claire while sleeping was taken to the world of dreams and there she saw her friend the she-wolf, she stretched out her hands to touch its hairy shoulders, the beast smiled and told her to stay alert, that she was coming home, that piece of information confused Claire, she asked which home, the beast only repeated its earlier information that she was coming home and that Claire should wait for her. As Claire stared blankly at her, the beast smiled and told Claire not to worry that the siege was almost over. Claire awoke from that dream and checked the wall clock hanging above her window, the time read five minutes to midnight, she scampered out of her bed and picked a blanket, she put her footwear underneath her arm to avoid making noise, then carefully she crept out of the house, the Duke had already gone up to his bed-chamber to sleep, si as Claire tiptoed towards the garden, only the knights on duty could be seen at the other end of the castle, she entered the garden, spread her thick blanket on the ground and waited for her friend. On second thought, she decided to check if the bottle was where she hid it, it wasn't there and Claire nearly had a heart attack, she searched frantically for it and yet couldn't find it, she was about to burst into tears when she went behind the flower hedge and found where the bottle tumbled to after it rolled out from where she hid it if she hadn't seen it that night, any servant or guard passing the next morning would have easily seen it since the bottle tumbled out of where it was hidden, if the wrong person had found it, the human bottled inside the wolf's body would be lost forever. She decided she was going to show the note and its content to the she-wolf when she arrived to see if the wolf would recognize it. At exactly the midnight hour, the howl of the beast was heard and once again the knights got ready to defend their lives. The beast leaped over the castle walls and headed straight towards the garden, just like it did the previous night. The knights looked at each other in wonder and exhaled once again with relief, it was obvious the beast didn't consider the knights worthy of her attention. As she walked straight towards the garden, her red hot eyes blazed ferociously and her tail swished gracefully in the air, though they were now friends yet the hairs on Claire's body stood with fright as the beast approached, as the beast came into view, Claire stretched her hands towards it in a friendly gesture, gradually the red hot color of the beast's eye dimmed and became as friendly as Claire remembered it, the she-wolf walked towards Claire and sat on its hind legs, Claire reached out and touched the hair on its body and the beast's face relaxed into the soothing friendly Claire loved.

"How have you been?" Claire asked the beast but of course, she got no answer.

The beast only rubbed its head with its paws and stared blankly at Claire

"Okay, I know you don't understand me but you sure can see me, so take a look at this, let's see if you recognize it."

Having said that, Claire turned and brought out the green bottle from where she kept it, the wolf took one look at it and suddenly let out a terrifying howl, its eyes suddenly blazed hot and red and it tried to reach for the bottle, Claire took some steps back in fear and stepped over a rough stone, the bottle dropped from Claire's shaky hands smashed on the granite stone lying there in the garden, instantly there was a mighty roar of thunder, Claire screamed and covered her ears, the knights on duty bravely held each other's hand wondering what was coming. The witch still cuddled in Winthrop's arms jerked up that instant for she perceived a magical reaction somewhere outside the castle, she jumped out of bed even as Winthrop reached for her, she kissed Winthrop on his lips and told him not to worry that she would be back soon,

"Can i visit you at the caves?" Winthrop asked the witch.

He couldn't believe he just asked the Duke that question but his heart wouldn't let him keep quiet, somehow as they made love, the witch found her way into his heart and refused to bulge. Put in simpler terms, Winthrop had fallen in love with the dreaded witch of the Zazu empire, when she slept in his arms, he realized that he wanted her to sleep in his arms forever, the witch stared at Winthrop in shock, did he just say he wanted to visit, no man ever wanted to visit her except people who urgently needed her help for she was seen as a horrible witch and nothing more, she never thought a sane man would want her, for the first time in several years, the witch caught herself crying, she returned to the bed, hugged Winthrop real tight and assured him that he could visit as much he liked, Winthrop smiled like a child receiving a new present and returned the witch's hug, then the witch left the room without looking back not even once, for she could feel her heart softening towards the youth on the bed. Again the sky rumbled with thunder, as the witch stepped into the cast sitting room, she nearly collided with the Duke who was descending hastily from upstairs, he was dressed in his nightwear and looked very frightened.

"I think something is wrong." that was all the witch said to Gastard before stepping into the night.

In the garden, Claire watched with horror as the wolf convulsed repeatedly like it was going to die, Claire heard the snap of bones and wondered what was wrong, then the hairs on the beast started falling off, that was too much for Claire, so she started screaming before her very eyes she saw the hard animal nails in the beast's falling off and in its place was human nails, Claire's eyes bulged in profound shock, the beast fell on its knees and started to transform into a lovely damsel, that was the last straw for Claire so she fainted, when she awoke she saw the witch, Gastard and princess Nirvena staring down at her. Though she was weary from her faint, she jumped up on seeing princess Nirvena and grabbed her hands excitedly, then suddenly she remembered that princess Nirvena was the beast that transformed before her eyes.

"So, it was you" Claire said in tears, the witch and Gastard just stared with their mouths wide open. Princess Nirvena ran into the arms of her best friend and together they wept like their hearts would break, suddenly the witch turned and hurried back to the castle, she went straight to her room and started packing her bags while Winthrop anxiously asked her what was wrong, the witch said nothing, si Winthrop dressed up too and decided he was going to follow her back to her six caves. And so it happened that while the Duke stood transfixed staring at his sister in absolute shock, the witch followed by her new love, under the cover of darkness ran back to the safety of her caves, no guard or knight dared stop her as she and Winthrop marched into the night.

CHAPTER FIFTEEN

5. Finally I'm home ancestors

No longer I'm I a visitor

In the home of my birth and succor

I take my place with candor

10. The tyrant is down

The grand fuckaholic and naughty clown

"You disgust me," princess Nirvena said to the Duke.

The knights had drawn close as they heard voices, on seeing princess Nirvena they embraced her with immense joy, within seconds the whole castle was astir with people, the princess was home and standing right in their midst.

"Where have you been?" everyone asked Princess Nirvena at once.

Aunt Marvy who held May protectively in her arms heard the hullabaloo and hurriedly dressed to go see for herself, May followed her too. On seeing the princess, her Aunt rushed and scooped her into her arms, she had nursed princess Nirvena when she was a baby and her disappearance so deeply wounded her spirit that she carefully avoided mentioning her name ever since she arrived in Zazu because talking about the princess brought back afresh the pain of her disappearance but now, right at the garden stood her lost baby, Aunt Marvy enclosed the princess in another warm hug as they both cried freely. One of the guards climbed the ladder that led to where a huge bell was suspended and rang it three consecutive times joyously, it was an ancient signal, which told the Zazu empire that there was a celebration at the castle, the practice was that the nearest province to the castle would hear the bell ring thrice and ring their province bell thrice also, the next province would do same until all provinces got the good news. While all these were going on, the Duke stood in complete shock not saying a word.

"But where is the beast?" a knight asked.

"I was the beast" princess Nirvena answered and a hush fell on all those gathered. "My brother, your so-called Duke and the nameless witch turned me into a beast several winters ago just because my brother wanted my throne, when our father was dying, he chose me as his successor for he disliked the meanness of my brother's heart. It is the duke's right to appoint his successor, when my father chose me, my brother became an enemy. Our father instructed him to gather all the Lords of the empire and crown me queen on my twenty-second birthday, our empire's prime Minister, lord Winston was there also when our father gave him the instruction, I'm glad lord Winston is still alive to confirm my words, one night my brother and the nameless witch barged into my room and turned me into a beast. I roamed the wild forest for months, for my human instincts were suspended, I had the crazy instincts of a beast and lived under the snow and sunshine, eating the slimy insects of the forest and...... " Princess Nirvena could say no more, she burst into tears and everyone listening to her wept along with her except Gastard whose head was bowed in shame.

"Thank you, Claire, for freeing my soul," Princess Nirvena said to Claire, they huffed each other crying freely, it was then it dawned on Claire that the beast was her best friend, little wonder she felt strongly pulled towards the wolf.

Claire was glad that she was instrumental to the freedom of her childhood friend, her first love, the very friend she had her first make out with years ago behind one of the tall hedges of the royal garden. Claire caught princess Nirvena staring at her lovingly and blushed bright red, the maids rushed princess Nirvena and took her into the castle for a good bath, she was home and they were determined to give her royal treatment. She was bathed vigorously in a scented bath, her teeth and tongue were scoured with the cleansing powder produced by Zazu's finest physicians until her teeth sparkled like the insides of coconut. Her hair which was tangled and rough was combed out, her nails which grew rough and coarse courtesy of her days in the wild forests were cut and polished until they shone bright pink. The castle maids loved princess Nirvena and they took adequate care of her. The chefs were not left out, that same late hour, they re-entered the kitchen and started cooking a feast that befits royalty, their princess had suffered starvation for months in the wild forests and the chefs were determined to make it up to her. While all these were happening, Claire was very close to princess Nirvena for she feared the princess would disappear again, the princess also desperately needed Claire close for they had missed each other. Before the disappearance of the princess, Claire and the princess were best of friends, a friendship that started when they were children, as they grew up, the love deepened but they were afraid to acknowledge their feelings because they feared the reaction of the people but Aunt Marvy's bold love affair with May told Claire that she had the right to love and she resolved to follow her heart and stay true to her nature. As the princess had a wash Claire stuck to her like a second skin, while she ate at the dining hall, Claire was there and when the princess was overtaken by sleep, it was in Claire's room downstairs that she slept for her room upstairs was locked and need intensive cleaning before it would become hospitable. That night, the princess lay on Claire's bosom and shed tears of relief, she was no longer a beast of the fields at the mercy of the elements rather she was returned to her lovely human nature, a state she thought she would never enjoy again until the hour of her death. She clung to Claire and Claire to her. Before the break of dawn, the castle was filled to the brim with the people of Zazu who wanted to confirm the rumor that their princess was well and alive. The castle guards opened the vast conference hall of the empire, it was a vast hall that could seat a thousand people, the throne of the Duke was at an elevated platform in the hall but the seat was empty. The people were ushered into the hall while the royal chefs stormed the kitchen to prepare as many pots of coffee as possible for the people. The instant Aunt Marvy woke up, she ran to Claire's room to check on her niece, she saw the princess cuddled safely in Claire's arms, instinctively she perceived the strong chemistry between them and smiled triumphantly, she could see her niece finding love in a fellow woman just like she did. Aunt Marvy approved completely for she believed that love can come from any gender and everyone should be free to love, looking at the two young girls who were sleeping soundly, Aunt Marvy could picture an ideological revolution sweeping through the whole Zazu empire and extending to other kingdoms, a revolution that would allow people of the same gender to love in peace. The moment the princess woke up, she ran to the window in excitement, she was glad to be alive and whole, she ran back to the bed and looked lovingly at Claire her best friend, love and soulmate, she gently kissed Claire's lips and then ran out to greet everyone, she was glad to be home. When the people of Zazu heard that their princess was awake, they demanded to see her instantly and so once again the princess was taken to the bathroom for another bath, she gladly followed the maids for she had missed her scented bath. When she was all dressed, she confidently marched down to the conference hall to see her people and once again Claire was beside her because the princess insisted on having Claire with her. Nobody bothered to ask about the Duke who locked himself upstairs and refused to come down. The princess narrated to the people how she was turned into a beast by her brother and the nameless witch because of the throne her father left for her. At this juncture in her story, the people of Zazu cheered wildly, they never liked Gastard, never wanted him, so on hearing that princess Nirvena was the successor the late Duke chose, they cheered heartily. Lord Winston, the prime Minister of the empire confirmed the princess story for he was there when the princess was chosen as successor, he only crowned Gastard because the late Duke said he was to manage the throne as regent until his sister's twenty-second birthday and when the princess went missing, lord Winston in accordance with the sacred custom of Zazu empire decided that Gastard would continue as Duke but thankfully the princess was home, safe and sound. She would be twenty - two the next month which meant that the Lords of Zazu had a coronation to plan.

Of all the people of Zazu who rejoiced at Gastard's disgrace, Lord Henry was the happiest, he would never forgive Gastard for breaking into his most sacred chamber and screwing blind his wife. Claire's parents too celebrated Gastard's fall from grace, finally, they could visit their daughter. The princess' return was an open door to so many people who were disgraced and oppressed by Gastard, the young princess boldly took over the affairs of the empire as Gastard remained locked up in his room and would speak to no one, all pleas from Aunt Marvy to get him out at least proved abortive. Gastard considered his life finished, he wanted to end his life and decided he wasn't going to die alone and so while he locked himself up, he planned on how to take the princess with him to the grave. When the Lords led by lord Winston brought a resignation letter to Gastard, he refused to come down from his self-imposed imprisonment and sign. Ge hadn't the face to look at anyone, his heart burned with hatred for his sister. To make matters worse for Gastard, when king Arthur heard of Gastard's disgrace and the safe return of the princess, he sent beautiful gifts congratulating the princess and wishing her a happy coronation in advance, sir Hareton king Arthur's general whose daughter Gastard fucked also sent princess Nirvena gifts, congratulating her on upcoming coronation. Gastard heard all these from his room upstairs for that was all the servants discussed besides Aunt Marvy always gave him details of the happenings in the empire hoping he would come out of his chamber and make things right. He never did. Meanwhile, the love between Claire and the princess deepened that when Claire packed and decided to go back to her family, the princess went down on her knees and begged Claire to stay by her side, she reminded Claire that they nearly lost each other once and should never be separated again, that was more than enough persuasion for Claire, she happily stayed back, besides the princess would need help to plan her coronation. Two weeks before the coronation of the princess as queen, the nameless witch followed by Winthrop who was healthier and happier entered the castle one morning and demanded to see the princess, the knights bravely barred her way, they had taken enough rubbish from the witch, the same crazy witch who Was responsible for turning the princess into a hideous wolf, there Was no way they were going to allow her to see the soon to be queen, not even from a mile away but Winthrop convinced the knights that the witch had come to make amends, unlike the Duke who hardened his heart. As convincing as Winthrop sounded, the knights weren't letting down their guard, so they told the witch to give them her message so that they would safely relay it to the princess. While the exchange was going on, the princess poked her head out of her room window which overlooked the courtyard, immediately the witch sighted the princess, she fell on her knees in total humility, which shocked everyone, the witch wasn't known to kneel before anyone. Right there on her knees, she promised the princess that she had turned a new leaf and as a sign of repentance, she was going to turn back to normal, all those she turned into hideous things, including the youth she turned into a giant penis. The witch said she would cancel all those terrible spells the next day and would like the people of Zazu to be present at the great conference hall of the royal castle. She swore by all the gods and goddesses she served that the people of Zazu had nothing to fear for she had found love, had come to appreciate the virtues of giving love and peace, and was a changed person. The princess had a gut feeling that the witch was telling the truth for the first time in her life, when the witch turned and left followed closely by her heartthrob Winthrop, the princess ordered that a circular be passed to all the provinces that the witch had an apology to make to the whole empire. The next morning, before the full break of dawn, the brave ones who wanted to hear what the witch had to say gathered at the castle's conference hall and waited for the witch. In the nick of time, the witch entered the hall, pulling before her a huge cart that contained numerous tied sacks and as usual, Winthrop was very much with her, a lot of persons lost their nerves on seeing her and stood up to run for their lives but the witch prostrated before the people pleading for pardon that was a new one for the books, so the people though still reasonably afraid went back to their seats. The witch proceeded to display her sorcery tools while the people murmured, afterward she looked around for the princess but didn't see her, the reason was simple, the people of Zazu didn't want their princess at close quarters with the witch ever again. Once bitten they say, twice shy. But Aunt Mary and Claire were very much present; they wanted to see for themselves and report accurately back to the princess. The witch began her incantations, she brought out a snail from a sack in the cart and made scary incantations over it, a great smoke arose around the witch and the people were stunned to see a young boy where the snail previously was. The mother of the boy screamed with joy, ran up to her child, and scooped him up, the boy had gone missing two years ago. All those whose loved ones were missing waited with intense anticipation as hideous creatures were turned back to their original human form, there was great jubilation in the conference for an unforgettable event that had occurred before their very eyes, and families were once again reunited with their long lost loved ones. The jubilation went off the roof when the huge penis was turned back to the youth who peeked at the witch while she had her bath. Yet, the dramatic turn of the penis back to human wasn't the ultimate drama of the day, the witch declared that she would like all Zazu people to know that she no longer had six caves but five for the sixth one was a human turned to rock, she declared that she had turned the rock back its original form, the woman whose husband was turned to rock rushed home for she knew he would be home waiting. After the great display of sorcery and Unbridled magic, the witch went down on her knees to apologize again but the people assured her that she was forgiven, she promised that never again will she use her magic prowess to hurt others but that she would henceforth use it for the good of the empire and wherever else help was needed. She walked away from the conference hall and for the first time, no one ran away from her, by that the witch knew she was forgiven. Holding firmly to Winthrop's hand they walked away, the news of the sorcery spread across all kingdoms and the vast seas. Aunt Marvy reported the news back to Gastard and urged him once again to make amends but Gastard said nothing he only requested for coffee and toast bread.

The princess coronation day dawned, bright and sunny but first the princess had a task she must perform, she walked into Claire's room, took Claire's hand and asked Claire to be hers forever. Claire's eyes filled with tears at the princess' words.

"Please, take my hand Claire and together we will convince the whole of Zazu and the world at large that love is sweet even if it is between women."

Claire ran into the princess' arms and they kissed passionately, suddenly they heard Gastard's voice behind them, he brandished a very sharp blade and told them to keep still, the princess tried to talk him out of his foolishness but he refused to listen, his intent was to stab the princess to death so that she would never sit on the throne of Zazu, as he approached, the princess retreated, a guard passing heard tense voices inside Claire's room and peeked cautiously inside, ge saw the terrible Duke pointing a blade at the soon to be coronated queen, without hesitation, the guard jumped on Gastard and wrestled the blade from him, he was bundled upstairs to his room and locked up, that was where he stayed until the entire empire led by Lord Winston gathered to crown the princess as the new Zazu queen. When the great royal trumpets blew announcing queen Nirvena's ascension to the sacred throne of Zazu, Gastard was filled with dreadful envy, he climbed out of his room and standing on the window of his room jumped to his death.

When he crashed below, a guard ran to the scene of the crash and saw a figure lying on the hard paved floor, he took a closer look and screamed in shock as he beheld the body of the Duke or better still what remained of his body. Gastard's brains were splattered gruesomely on the hard floor, the left part of his face was battered beyond recognition, before long loads of people started gathering around the body and surprisingly nobody thought of crying, perhaps they didn't see enough reason to cry, then someone with authority came, a young knight, people made way for him as he approached the body of the former Duke, just as the knight bent down to wrap the body of Gastard with a thick blanket, lord Henry whispered something into his ears and the knight nodded, the body of the late Duke was wrapped up as the Lords of Zazu approached the scene followed by the newly coronated queen Nirvena. The body was taken to one of the empty rooms in the castle for.

When the new queen was informed of her brother's death, she wept bitterly for though he was a total jerk while he lived, he was still her brother and she loved him, his flaws, perfection and all, the Lords as the body was been taken to the embalming room doffed their caps in honor of the fallen royalty, no one except the new queen really mourned him, lord Henry tried hard not to smile, he wasn't sorry not even in the least way, as a matter of fact he was plotting a good strategy that would help him cut off the penis of the late Gastard, that penis had screwed his wife mercilessly and defiled the hollowness of his secret chamber, his wife was a temple he alone was permitted to worship in, Gastard while he lived broke into that temple and worshiped aggressively without fear, lord Henry was determined to get that randy penis and cut it to several pieces after which he would bury it, that was a crazy thing to do but that was the only vengeance that would give him joy and heal his bruised ego. According to the sacred traditions of the empire, after the coronation of a new empire, the next day there was always a grand party where other monarchs from other kingdoms would come together and celebrate with the new emperor but because of Gastard's tragic death, the party was canceled temporarily. A physician was brought to embalm the body ahead of a state burial but the physician was shocked to discover that within the minutes it took him to arrive at the castle, Someone had cut off the penis and balls of the late Gastard, that wasn't all, while the empire wondered who cut off those balls some ladies came claiming that they were pregnant for the late Gastard and they were ready to swear. They did swear by the portions of the nameless witch and the whole of Zazu was convinced that Gastard even in death had fathered children. The queen took the responsibility for these women for they were royalty even though their ties with the royal family occurred under very dramatic circumstances. On the day Gastard was buried, it was difficult to find a teary eye as only the queen wept, he was buried in the tomb of his ancestors and Zazu had peace.

With Gastard's mourning and burial safely out of the way, a celebration day was fixed for the new queen, all monarchs of all surrounding kingdoms were present, even the Amerian prince crossed the vast sea to attend and honor the new queen, together these royalties blessed queen Nirvena's staff of office and wished her a prosperous reign, that was queen Nirvena's moment and she so seized it, she drew Claire to herself and kissed her passionately in the presence of all, at first there was a massive hush and then king Arthur started clapping, soon a few others joined in and suddenly everyone was cheering the queen.

Love had won.